fishing

500

D0174932

I

LEGENDS OF THE OUTER BANKS AND TAR HEEL TIDEWATER

Other books by Charles H. Whedbee

The Flaming Ship of Ocracoke
and Other Tales of the Outer Banks

Outer Banks Mysteries
and Seaside Stories

Charles Harry Whedbee

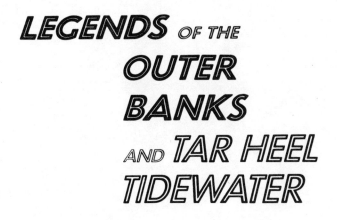

LEGENDS OF THE OUTER BANKS AND TAR HEEL TIDEWATER

illustrated by Anne Kesler Shields

JOHN F. BLAIR, *Publisher*
Winston-Salem 1966

Thirteenth Printing, 1989

TO *RACHEL*

FOREWORD

*You are handed herewith a small pod or school of leg-*ends about various portions of that magical region known as the Outer Banks of North Carolina as well as stories from other sections of the broad bays, sounds, and estuaries that make up tidewater Tarheelia.

Many of the inhabitants of these storm-swept shore lines are living legends in themselves. Others have gone on to their reward, leaving us the poorer for their passing. It is to try to preserve some of the folklore and legend which they knew so well and told so vividly that this little volume is attempted.

These legends fall naturally into three classes. The first class contains tales that the writer knows are true because he was there when and as the events occurred. The second group of stories he believes to be true because they were told and retold to him by upright and honest people whose reputations for veracity have been unimpeachable and who obviously believe the stories themselves. The third class is composed of tales that, it seems, are impossible of verification or of refutation.

Certainly this last class contains at least the germ or seed of truth.

For obvious reasons, no effort will be made to point out which legend falls within which class. The reader might well be misled if this were attempted; and, besides, it would not be nearly so much fun. This much can be said: a good portion of these legends has a solid basis in fact.

Charles Harry Whedbee
Whalebone Junction
Nag's Head, North Carolina

CONTENTS

LEGENDS OF THE
OUTER
BANKS
AND *TAR HEEL*
TIDEWATER

1
THE RIDDLE OF SHALLOTTE INLET

There is a fascination about sea water which continues to intrigue laymen and doctors alike. Almost any competent chemist can tell you that water from the open sea is almost identical with human blood in its chemical make-up. Evolutionists claim that life originated in the sea, migrating onto land first as amphibian creatures capable of breathing either air or water, and evolving later as breathers of air alone. Certainly the sea is the last great frontier on this earth, which man is only just beginning to explore and understand.

When Ponce de León came to this country, one of his prime objects was to find the so-called Fountain of Youth, a magical upwelling or stream of water that Indian legend claimed had the power to restore lost youth. Since Ponce de León's journal never mentions finding the Fountain of Youth, we must assume that he never claimed to have located it. There are several references, however, to another stream that the Indians volunteered to show him—a stream with healing qualities, where infections, fevers, and "vapors" were cured simply by bathing in its magical waters.

It is probable that Ponce was much more interested in gold and other treasures than he was in any healing waters. At any rate, there is no evidence that he even looked for this stream (although he did consider it of sufficient interest to justify a memorandum or two). This watercourse was supposed to lie to the northward and to be at the end of a journey of many suns' duration.

Rather far to the northward of de León's country, certainly a distance it would have taken many suns to travel by foot or canoe, there lies a portion of North Carolina s Outer Banks within the boundaries of Brunswick County that is known as Shallotte's Inlet. This inlet is a most peculiar phenomenon. It can, and it does, cure infection, responsible people say. It can, and it does, heal old wounds that have festered and "wept" for long periods of time. It can and does cure several other types of disease to which the human flesh is heir.

Many people in Brunswick County think that these are the Indians' legendary healing waters. Included among the people who believe sincerely in the medicinal qualities of this stream are several medical doctors and a number of chemists. It is an open secret that intensive research in both qualitative and quantitative chemistry is going on even now to try to solve the riddle of these waters.

Several of the doctors came to these tide-swept regions to scoff but remained with widened and incredulous eyes to learn more about it. There definitely is something in this water that is not in other water. Too many people who were ill and infected have recovered after bathing here—and with no other type of treatment—for the phenomenon to be explainable as mass hysteria. Indeed, several of the most dramatic cures have occurred, it is said, because the affected parties fell accidentally into these waters. Old-time bear hunters have known about the spa for years. It is averred that many a good bear dog owes his life to the curative powers of this flow because he was dumped into it, sink or swim, after being injured by his quarry.

Shallotte's Inlet is located about seven miles from the lovely little town of Shallotte on the southern end of the Outer Banks. Quite near Holden's Beach, it is readily accessible and even appears on most road maps of the region. The Inlet is a part of the famous Inland Waterway; and, though much of it is under federal control, all of it is open to the public.

Present in this particular watercourse is a peculiar type of rush or reed that grows nowhere else, so far as is known, but grows here in abundance. In the center of the reed is found a substance that looks for all the world like bread. At last report the growth had not been pinned down other than being generally classified as of the genus *Juncus* in the family *Juncaceae*. It is thought, however, that this plant is not unique to Shallotte's Inlet. Such a thing would be a rarity, indeed, in botany.

It has been definitely established, however, by careful observation and repeated experiment, that when these reeds become inundated with salt water from the sea, as frequently happens, a sort of mould develops on the breadlike substance and then washes off in large quantities until the water in the vicinity assumes a rather milky appearance. It is this milky water which has been present in all cases where infectious ailments and other ills have been reported as cured.

Science may try to explain that this is some sort of natural penicillin factory, or perhaps that there are other and even more powerful penicillin-like drugs which are formed by the interaction of the sea water with the bready segments of the reeds. Indian legend, on the other hand, insists that these are, indeed, magical waters provided by the Great Spirit for the comfort and healing of His people.

Do you think this is only an old wives' tale? If so, you will be delighted to learn that the people of the section are quite willing to talk about it. Just ask any of the native-born sons or daughters of Shallotte or, for that matter, of Calabash, Grissettown, Olyphic, or Makatoka, North Carolina. Chances are he can point to a living member of his own family who has bathed in these healing waters and has been cured. You are not really entitled to a single hoot until you have first checked the facts for yourself.

2
THE GHOST DEER OF ROANOKE

Since time immemorial and up to the beginning of the
twentieth century, the Outer Banks of the Old North
State were remarkable for a profusion of grapevines.
There is something about the air and about the minerals
in the soil that seems to grow beautiful grapes on luxuriant vines. There was a time within the memory of men
still living when the grapes grew down so close to the
sea that the very ocean swells would break upon them
in time of storm. It was great sport for the more daring
of the young boys in that section to grasp a stout grapevine and swing, Tarzan-like, out over the ocean shallows. Roanoke Island, itself, was partially covered with
these vines.

One of the very oldest of these grapevines grew on
the eastern shore line of that island. It had a main stem
as big as a man's body, and the place where it grew was
known over many parts of the world as the Mother
Vineyard. Slips or cuttings from this Mother Vineyard
were carried to England and to France and there planted
and tended. Many of the slips are said to have been car-

ried to California, where they grew, and still grow, in great profusion.

Up until a few years prior to this writing, this Mother Vineyard was kept on a reduced scale, and some very excellent wine was made from its grapes. The name is still carried on some of the highway signs on Roanoke Island, but most of the vineyard has now given way to a very beautiful housing project on the shore line of this storied island. The subdivision is now known by the name of the Mother Vineyard. *Sic transit gloria.*

Captain Martin Johnson, who used to run the steamer *Trenton* from Elizabeth City to Nag's Head and Manteo in the early nineteen-twenties, knew the ancient legend of that vine. It was a reverie-inducing fable he would tell to the children of the passengers of his fine craft to while away some of the long hours as the *Trenton* churned her way through the cola-colored waters of Albemarle Sound. I heard the same legend related many years ago as a group of smallish boys sat around a campfire on the banks of a broad river where the Matchapungo Indians once had a town. Talk about goose bumps and furtive looks into the dark forest beyond the fire's circle of light!

The story begins in the time when the John White settlers first came to Roanoke in the year 1587. As you know, Virginia Dare was born, both she and Chief Manteo were baptized into the Christian faith, and Governor White set sail for England to bring back supplies but was unable to return for three full years.

According to the legend, in the autumn of the second year of the City of Raleigh, hostile savages under Chief Wanchese attacked the city and the fort. There had been many disputes by Wanchese and his followers with the leaders of the colonists. The fact that Governor White did not return as he had promised caused Wanchese to believe that the colony had been deserted, and he grew more insolent as the months went by. Finally the chief swore a great oath to kill every colonist, down to the last woman and child, and thus rid his island of the hated foreigners. Retribution was not to be feared from the men in the "great canoes with wings" since they had obviously forgotten this little band. So it was that Wanchese sat down and planned the complete destruction of the white settlement and the murder of all its inhabitants.

The raiders attacked at dawn and without warning. Several of the colonists were killed before they could reach the safety of the fort, but those within that rude battlement managed to close the doors and set up an answering fire with their muskets. Thus the siege of Fort Raleigh began. Poisoned arrows were used by Wanchese's warriors, and every time a settler showed himself atop the fort, he was the immediate target for those deadly missiles. With the approach of night, fire arrows were brought into play. In the twilight many buildings within the enclosure became flaming torches illuminating the desperate scene. Not knowing how long they could hold out and wanting to conserve their water for drinking purposes, the colonists attempted to take down the buildings that were afire and thus prevent the flames from spreading while they replied with musket shot to the onslaughts of the Indians.

Chief Manteo had been on a fishing expedition that day, and Wanchese believed he would remain away for several days at the very least. The friendly Indian had taken a small party of his tribe and had gone southward in the direction of Hatteras. He had found fishing no good at all and was returning in the dusk when he saw the red glow in the sky.

Sensing trouble from so large a blaze, he redoubled his speed; and as he drew near the fort, he began to hear the sounds of musket fire as well as the shrill, wild cry of the war-crazed attackers. Trouble had been brewing for some time with the dissident braves under the other chief's command, and Manteo at once grasped what was happening. He realized that his small fishing party was badly outnumbered by the Indians whom he could see leaping and screaming in the light of the burning buildings. Knowing full well that the colonists could not last until he went for reinforcements, he determined to try to help them escape.

Gaining entrance to the fort by a secret tunnel which opened on the banks of the Sound, Manteo and his small band urged the colonists to flee under cover of darkness while yet they could. This they did. There was no time to bury their dead and no time to take more than the most meager personal belongings. Hurriedly the survivors crept single file through the tunnel and down to the shore where the canoes of the fishing party were waiting.

As Ananias and Eleanor Dare with their infant daughter, Virginia, followed Manteo through the dense woods which screened the tunnel's mouth, Ananias bethought him of the agreement with Governor White that the colonists would carve the name of their destination on a tree if they had to flee Fort Raleigh. Thereby, rescue parties could the more easily find them.

Over Manteo's strong protest, Ananias insisted on stopping before a great oak tree. He whipped out his sheath knife, quickly stripped the bark off a portion of the oak about head-high, and began to carve upon the bared surface. Three letters only did he carve, *C R O*, when a lone straggler from Wanchese's attacking force saw him and, with a triumphant scream, shot a poisoned arrow through his heart, killing him on the spot. The return fire from Manteo's bow came only a split second later. It, too, was fatal, killing the attacker in his tracks and gaining a few more seconds of precious time before the besiegers would find that their quarry was escaping.

Fearful that this new commotion might bring others of the attacking force, Manteo now insisted on immediate flight. At first Eleanor Dare was reluctant to leave the body of her fallen husband. It was not until Manteo reminded her of her duty to the infant, Virginia, that she tearfully agreed to go. To reassure her, the noble chief made the sign of the cross upon his own forehead and with his finger made the same sign on the forehead of the infant. Then, lifting his eyes to the sky, he pledged lifelong protection to the distraught mother and her baby.

Swiftly now they made their way to the waiting canoes, as swiftly boarded them, and pushed off into the night. The strong arms of Manteo and of his companions at the paddles sped them on into the trackless expanse of water north of the Island. All night they traveled lest Wanchese's braves might pursue them in war canoes. As dawn was beginning to color the east, they came to the home of Manteo's people. Later that same day they were joined by the other survivors of the attack; and, falling down in the wigwams of their rescuers, they slept the sleep of exhaustion. For the time being, their lives were safe. No force of Wanchese was strong enough to attack this village.

The next day a great council was held. Manteo called together the subchiefs of his people and pleaded with them to receive the white people into the tribe as their own. The Indian women, meanwhile, were much taken with little Virginia Dare. They could not understand her fair, white skin, and they seemed fascinated by it. She was not sun-tanned like the other colonists, and she was not red-skinned like the Indians. Moreover, her hair was a soft golden color, such as they had never seen on mortal being. "Little snow-papoose" they called her and wondered among themselves whether she would melt away with the return of the summer sun as the snow did.

The council heeded Manteo's plea and agreed to accept the white colonists into the tribe as blood brothers. Small cuts were made in the arms of each of the whites and of a corresponding number of Indians. Then the arm of each colonist was bound to the arm of his Indian counterpart and the blood permitted to mingle so that they did, indeed, become blood brothers. After only a few minutes the bonds were cut and the arms freed. Thus did necessity make Indians of them all.

With the practicality of people who live close to nature, the first thing the red men did was to help these newcomers build wigwams of their own. Then they taught the whites to hunt the red deer and to fish for the great fish that swam in the sounds and bays. All this and much more the people of Manteo's tribe taught the colonists. The new arrivals, for their part, taught the Indians about the white man's God and about Christ and His compassion for all people. In time they also taught them how to build a two-story house, a thing never before heard of by the Indians. The colonists also instructed their hosts in the use of a musket and showed them how to read or "speak from a book," as well as how to use crossbows, breastplates, and helmets. All in all, it was an exchange of vast benefit to both sides, and the adopted members fitted well into the life of the tribe.

The child, Virginia Dare, was the marvel and the cynosure of all the Indians. As she grew into young womanhood, her character and her personality developed to equal her great beauty, and she became the favorite of all who knew her. With her fair complexion, deep blue eyes, and hair the color of wild honey, she soon became a sort of white priestess to them. "Winona-Ska" they called her, and they listened intently as she told them of her mother's homeland and its ways and of her belief in God and His mercy to all His children. Her most difficult task was to teach them not to worship her, for this they were most ready to do. They brought all their troubles to her and sought her aid in settling disputes. Her counsel was accepted by them on all manner of things. On many occasions she settled the most bitter arguments simply by appearing on the scene and, with an admonitory hand, making the sign of the cross over them.

All the braves of Manteo's tribe loved Winona-Ska. They brought her presents of red deer and foxes and delicious fish which they speared in the sounds. One of them, however, outdid all the others in his devotion and in his tireless efforts to please her. This was Okisko, a brave of noble blood who was only a year or two her senior but already one of the mightiest hunters of the tribe.

Being an Indian brave, he was troubled greatly by his belief that it would be unmanly to speak of his love, and yet he wanted most desperately to show this goddess-woman how he felt. Each day he tried in some new way to show his love yet never spoke of it. On one occasion he even tried to affix to his canoe the wings of a huge goose he had killed, hoping that he would thus be able to sail the small craft as she had told him her people sailed. With such magnificent wings on his canoe, he thought, he might sail a mighty journey eastward and find her people for her. Even though his fellow braves mocked him for this and for other similar acts, Okisko persisted in them, the only way he knew to show his love.

Winona-Ska, with a woman's insight, saw immediately what was going on, and she realized what the situation was. She was deeply touched. She liked Okisko very much but felt no love for him other than she might have felt for a brother, had she been lucky enough to have one. And with an insight beyond his sex and beyond his years, Okisko contented himself with waiting. His hope and his belief was that someday love would awaken within the heart of Winona-Ska and that she would then turn to him as her choice for a mate.

The fair beauty of Winona-Ska was not lost on others

of the tribe either. Old Chico, the magician and witch doctor, looked long and searchingly at her. As he gazed, his youth seemed to return; the fires of long-forgotten young manhood seemed to rekindle in his breast. Yes, he, too, loved this young maiden. He loved her in his own way, he wanted her as his squaw, and he set about to woo her. He would cover himself with bright war paint and place huge feathers on his head and arms. Thus decorated, he would strut and posture before her like some great, outlandish bird. He would make great magic by rattling dried melon seeds in a gourd and would dance fierce dances for what he hoped would be her pleasure.

Kindheartedly, Winona-Ska smiled upon his efforts but mostly to keep the others from laughing. Although old enough to be her father, Chico grew wildly jealous of her. When he would see her smile at the young Okisko, his very soul would burn with jealousy and rage. Sick with desire and hopelessness, he finally determined that, if he could not have her as his wife, then no man would.

Although he had not had occasion to use his knowledge of magic in recent years, Chico had been a great magician in his day. He knew all the ancient spells handed down from his great-grandfather, who had also been the great-grandfather of the evil Wanchese. Chico knew the language of the lost spirits and could communicate with them. It was even rumored he could talk with the Evil One Himself. The old medicine man also knew many sinister potions and supernatural recipes whereby man might control a part of nature itself, and it was this course that he finally decided to pursue. By the use of his own black magic, he would once and for all insure that Winona-Ska would be his, or else she would be no man's.

With a great deal of effort Chico set about collecting from the waters as many pearls from the abundant mussels as he could find. Not ordinary pearls, mind you. For his dark purpose he required pied or speckled pearls which seemed to glow like fireflies with their own eerie light and to emit a sort of purple incandescence. Such pearls are known by magicians to be the souls of water nymphs who have disobeyed the King of the Sea and, for punishment, have been sentenced to imprisonment in the shells of mussels. These water nymphs are very grateful when freed by mortal men, and they will do anything the liberator asks of them, whether the request be for good or for evil. When he had a sufficient number of these liberated nymphs under his control, Chico revealed his plan to them. He told them what he plotted to do to the golden Winona-Ska and demanded their help in his scheme as the price of their freedom. True to their natures and obligated to him for freeing them, they promised to help him.

This being accomplished, Chico hid his pied pearls and set about to build a large canoe. He fashioned it with great care, so that it floated with grace upon the waters like a large swan. It was a beautiful vessel. When it was finished, he asked Winona-Ska to take a trip with him to Roanoke so that the canoe could be blessed by the spirits there. He assured her that the trip could be made within a few hours and that, if they left at dawn, they would return long before the evening cooking fires were lit. Although she had been back to these scenes of her early childhood many times, Winona-Ska agreed to go with Chico to keep from hurting his feelings. After all, the weather was beautiful, the water was calm, and the canoe was a new and fine one. She was flattered to be asked to take the first trip in such a handsome craft.

Now, indeed, was Chico's plot working to perfection. Although the sea nymphs have no power on water—for there the Sea King is the absolute ruler—once on land, their powers are tremendous, and their magic is so fierce that only a greater magic can withstand it. Thus Chico had schemed to get his beautiful prey to go with him across the water and then to land a good distance from their village, so that no one might be near to witness the evil deed he had in mind.

Chico had sung and chanted to each of his speckled pearls and had bathed them in a magic potion. He had then strung them into a lovely necklace, giving each pearl an explicit reminder of what he expected of her. As he and Winona-Ska glided over the water toward the island of Roanoke, he gave the necklace to her; and she, greatly pleasured by the beauty of his gift, placed the magic necklace around her neck. Unsuspecting, she fingered the pearls and looked at them in admiration, for they seemed to glow with their own light. She would, of course, give the lovely ornament back to Chico. It was too fine a gift to accept from one to whom she was not betrothed. For the time, though, she would wear it and enjoy its unreal beauty before giving it back on their return to the home village.

As they approached the sandy shores of Roanoke, Chico drove his paddle deep into the waters of the Sound and sent his new boat fairly flying over the calm surface, so that it ran half its length out upon the sandy shore before stopping. Lightfooted and happy, Winona-Ska sprang from the canoe and onto the sandy beach; and there, after leaving just one human footprint, she changed into a magnificent snow-white doe and sprang away into the forest.

Along the shores of that wooded island, the evil laughter of old Chico rang out and echoed back and forth among the pine and yaupon trees. Success was his! Winona-Ska had indeed now been placed far beyond the powers of any ordinary man to possess her. Thus was Chico's evil oath fulfilled.

Meanwhile, in the village the Indians waited long for Winona-Ska to return. No one had seen her leave with Chico, and Chico kept his own counsel. At his request, she had told no one of her plans lest such a disclosure spoil the blessing of the canoe. Far and wide the red men searched for their lost high priestess. Many and long were the journeys they made, but all in vain. Winona-Ska had vanished as though the very earth had swallowed her up. Finally the search was given up, and she was mourned as forever lost.

Shortly thereafter there began a legend of a strange white doe that roamed the woods of Roanoke. The other deer looked upon her as a sort of leader, the story went, and followed wherever she led. Furthermore, no arrow was able to kill, or even to hit, this white doe. Many braves coveted the white fur for a ceremonial robe, and some of the best hunters of several tribes had tried to kill her but in vain. She seemed to lead a truly charmed life.

When this became known, the older women of the

tribe began to put two and two together. Firm believers in witchcraft, they saw the similarity between the vanished white maiden and the sudden appearance of the white doe. Since they remembered that old Chico had been a great magician, they gossiped that it must have been Chico and his black magic that had caused the disappearance of the girl; that Chico must have bewitched Winona-Ska and changed her into a white doe. It takes only one repetition of gossip to change "it must have been" to "it was"; so was it with the aborigines then as it is with more civilized people now. By the third retelling it was being stated as a fact that Chico was responsible.

Okisko heard this gossip, and his heart was glad. He also readily accepted this explanation of the disappearance of his beloved. Since Winona-Ska had been bewitched, perhaps he could find even greater magic to break the spell. First, though, the white doe should be captured for her own protection and then the magical antidote searched for. In the days that followed, the young brave traveled often to Roanoke to try to capture the white doe but without any semblance of success. He could not even come close to capturing her. No matter how cunning his traps, she would always avoid them. It seemed as though she could read his mind. On several occasions when he caught sight of the splendid animal, she seemed to look directly at him with a great sorrow in her soft eyes before she turned and faded away into the forest.

Almost physically sick with frustration and believing now that he could never capture the white doe without the aid of a great magic, Okisko packed his canoe and traveled all the way to Weapomeoc, the Meeting of the Waters. Here was a great Indian settlement of Okisko's nation, which was the home of a mighty magician known as Wenaudon. Unknown to Okisko, there had long been bad feeling and much jealousy between the mighty Wenaudon and the wily Chico. Wenaudon was only too glad to be the instrument whereby his enemy might be embarrassed and made to look foolish. When he had heard Okisko's story, he immediately agreed to help him.

Taking Okisko aside into the forest where they could talk in secret, Wenaudon told him of a magic spring of water on Roanoke Island. It was a bubbling, natural fountain of fresh water where the sea nymphs held their revels and where they met their lovers. So enamoured were the nymphs of this spot that they had laid a spell upon the waters that would always make true lovers happy and secure. To drink of this magic spring was to have one's youth restored. He who bathed in the waters in the light of the full moon was given the power to undo all black magic and cancel out all evil spells. Having bathed in this spring when he was only an apprentice magician, Wenaudon knew of it, and he now prepared to share this knowledge with Okisko.

"First," he told his young visitor, "you must secure a tooth from the fierce hammerhead shark. It must be a long and narrow tooth, and very sharp. Then, within the triangle formed by the corners of this tooth, you must affix three purple mussel-pearls, one to each corner and each made bright with much rubbing and polishing. To this shark's tooth, you must affix an arrow shaft of witch-hazel wood that has never before been used as an arrow. To fletch this magic weapon, you must pluck just one feather from the wing of a living heron, then release the heron without further harm, and hide the arrow from all human sight. Let no one gaze upon it, and tell no one of your purpose. Then, when the moon is full, take the arrow from its hiding place and submerge it in the magic waters of the enchanted spring on Roanoke. There let it remain for three full nights while you stand guard. When the sun is rising on the third morning after its submerging, take the arrow in your hands thus and point it toward the rising sun. Pray the Great Spirit that your arrow may free the gentle Winona-Ska from the evil charm and restore her to you.

"With this arrow you must then hunt the white doe. When you have brought her to bay, take care to shoot the arrow straight into her heart. Do not fear. She will not be harmed by your arrow. If your aim is true, the evil spell of Chico will be ended, and she will resume her human form."

Thus spoke Wenaudon to Okisko, who heeded every word and wrote it upon his heart. The young lover then made haste to return to his native village and thence go to Roanoke, where he began the preparation of his magic arrow. Each step was followed with care, and the arrow was finally completed, exactly as he had been instructed.

It also happened that, at this same time, the neighboring chief, Wanchese, son of the old Chief Wanchese, called for a truce among all the tribes and announced a mighty hunt to celebrate the ending of hostilities. He proposed a smoking of the peace pipe among the nations and then a joint hunt, in which the quarry would be the fabled white doe of Roanoke. The brave who killed the white doe would be named the greatest hunter among them all.

Tired of senseless fighting, the other chiefs agreed, although they only half trusted the word of this younger Wanchese. They remembered too well the treachery of the old Chief Wanchese, his father; and they feared the son might be too much like the father. Since no harm could come from an attempt at peace, however, it was decided to go along with the young Wanchese's plan, keeping a sharp eye out all the while for any sign of betrayal.

Now, this young Wanchese had as a gift from his father a silver arrowhead which Queen Elizabeth herself had given him upon his visit to England. The young chief fully believed that this lustrous arrowhead held some magic power. He planned to use it to kill the white doe himself and thus bring to his tepee the fame and the glory that such a feat would ensure.

The hunt was duly organized, and only braves of noble blood were allowed to participate. On the appointed day the princely hunters took to the woods—Okisko with his magic arrow and Wanchese with his silver-pointed dart. Though neither knew the other was near, both these mighty hunters spied the white doe at the same instant. She was standing perfectly still and gazing at the ruins of the ancient Fort Raleigh. Aiming carefully and with bated breath, Okisko and Wanchese each drew his powerful bow and, at the same instant, shot his special arrow at the beautiful target at a range so close it seemed impossible that either could miss. One arrow carried with it hope, love, and compassion. The other bore malice, greed, and cunning. The hunters were equally skilled and equally powerful, and both arrows pierced the heart of the white doe, making the shape of a cross as they did so. As the fates would have it, Okisko's arrow arrived at the target just a split second before the dart of Wanchese.

To the amazement of Wanchese, a silver mist seemed to envelop the white doe as, before his very eyes, she changed from a doe to a beautiful young woman with long, golden hair and bright blue eyes.

To the anguish of Okisko, as soon as his beloved resumed her human form, there was the silver-headed arrow piercing her heart. From its wound the bright red blood flowed down the side of Winona-Ska. Restored to her human form one instant, but mortally wounded the next, she slowly collapsed and fell prostrate on the forest floor.

Wanchese fled in terror at this sight, but Okisko ran to his beloved. He found that his magic arrow had, indeed, pierced the heart of Winona-Ska but had done no harm and, as Wenaudon had predicted, had accomplished her transformation. Wanchese's arrow, arriving a heartbeat later, had pierced the human heart and had broken the shark's-tooth point of the magic arrow.

In one wild and desperate attempt yet to save his Winona-Ska, Okisko seized his broken arrow and ran headlong back along the forest trail until he reached the enchanted spring. Here, in broad daylight, he plunged his magic arrow into the bubbling fountain and besought the Great Spirit that his beloved be spared. As Okisko knelt and looked at the plashing waters, the spring began to subside and to disappear into the ground. Before his anguished eyes, it dried up and vanished com-

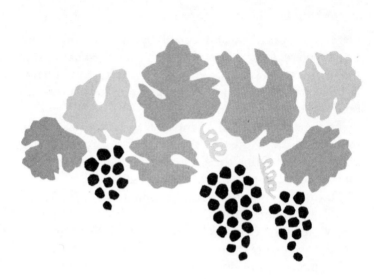

pletely. Simultaneously, the arrow became firmly rooted in the ground where the nymphs' enchanted spring had been. From the top and sides of the arrow, little green leaves began to appear. As they grew and unfolded before his eyes, they became the leaves of a grapevine, and the witch-hazel staff turned into the main stem of the vine. When he returned to look for his Winona-Ska near the ruins of the fort, she was nowhere to be seen; but yonder, in the gathering dusk, he thought he saw the flash of a white deer bounding away. At least a part of his prayer had been answered. The white doe was restored to life, but never again could she be transformed into her human form. To this day, she is said to roam the woods of Roanoke and of the mainland as well, as impervious to modern guns as she was to bows and arrows. To try in any way to harm her is said to bring on the worst fortune imaginable.

Over the years the grapevine grew and flourished, and the main stem became in time as thick as a man's body. Thus was the Mother Vineyard started, and thus was established the parent vine that has furnished slips and cuttings to be transplanted all over this country of ours, and in England and France as well.

It was claimed for years that, on a dark and moonless night, you could, if you listened very carefully, hear the lovely Winona-Ska crying for her lost love. There were even those who said that the blueness of some of the grapes was the very blueness in the eyes of that lovely maid who was born here many centuries before.

3
BEECHLAND

The mystery of the ultimate fate of the Sir Walter Raleigh colonists has fascinated and bemused historians for centuries. No human skeletons were found at the deserted town and fort on Roanoke Island. Only the single word *C R O A T O A N* carved on a tree and the letters *C R O* carved on a post nearby offered the slightest hint as to the fate of those brave settlers.

When Governor John White left the little colony in August, 1587, to return to England for supplies, all had seemed safe and serene. The Indians were friendly. Chief Manteo had visited England and the court of Queen Elizabeth and had later been baptized into the Christian faith. The governor's granddaughter, Virginia Dare, had been safely born and christened on Roanoke. All prospects indicated a quick and safe trip for John White and an early return to his colony.

Upon arriving in England some weeks later, White found queen and country in growing fear of invasion by the mighty Spanish Armada, the largest and seemingly most formidable naval force ever assembled up until that time. To permit ships to leave England in such a time of danger was unthinkable. In vain did White plead with Elizabeth to be allowed to take just one small ship with supplies for the New World colonists. That one small ship, however, might mean the difference between victory and defeat in the anticipated sea battle with Spain. No fraction of England's naval force must leave her in this time of peril.

In due time Spain's assault was made upon the island kingdom, the mighty Armada was cut to disorganized fragments by superb British seamanship, and England emerged as the dominant sea power of the age. From that day forward, Spain would be no more than a second-rate sea power.

With the Spanish threat repulsed and the danger of invasion gone, Queen Elizabeth gave immediate consent for the return of Governor White with British ships and supplies for the relief of the little colony on Roanoke. Three years had passed by then. What happened during those three years, how long the colonists endured before leaving, Governor White was unable to ascertain. When he returned in August, 1590, he conducted as thorough a search of the area as time and circumstances would permit. The occurrence of several severe storms just at this time and the anxiety of his ship captains to return to England in the face of such dangerous weather conditions cut short the search. We now know that this is the time of year when hurricanes begin to threaten, and it may be that the "severe storms" mentioned in his account were almost of hurricane destructiveness. At any rate, Governor White returned to England a broken-hearted and remorseful father and grandfather. As long as he lived, John White must have been tormented by

27

the recurring question in all his nightmares and in many of his waking moments, where were his daughter and his little granddaughter? Were they even alive? Did Manteo not protect them? Were they hungry tonight, or cold? Would the elders teach little Virginia about her grandfather, or was he forever accursed and forgotten by them as they must have felt forgotten by him? Why had he ever been a party to sending his daughter into that savage wilderness in the first place? If John White loved his daughter—and there is ample evidence that he did—these thoughts must have remained with him until his dying day.

The territory to the west of Roanoke Island was then, and remains today, some of the wildest and most inaccessible in this entire country of ours. Although there are settlements along the shore lines of the sounds and rivers, and although the adjacent waters are charted and are familiar to many, the land mass remains largely as wild and as unknown to man as the far side of the moon. Thousands upon thousands of acres remain upon which the foot of the white man has never trod. Was this region the ultimate destination of the Lost Colony? The very wildness and inaccessibility of it may have prevented the search and exploration that would have solved the mystery. A growing number of thoughtful people are inclining toward the view that it was and, in the light of fairly recent clues, are becoming excited about just such a possibility.

The historian Hakluyt, in Volume III of his painstaking history of the principal English voyages, quotes Governor White as having written: "For at my coming away [in August, 1587], they were prepared to re-move from Roanoak 50 miles into the maine."

Furthermore, Chief Manteo, the friendly Indian, was a member of the Matchapungo tribe. This tribe pos-sessed a territory that was, it seemed to them, ideally suited for the location of a permanent town or settle-ment. Here they had built a village which they are said to have called Croatoean. It was located approximately "50 miles into the maine" from the site of Fort Raleigh by the route that travelers making most of the journey on foot would, of necessity, have taken to get there. It was located on a creek that was, and still is, very deep, having, more than fifteen miles upstream from its mouth, an average depth of some 15 to 20 feet. Today this deep creek goes by the name of Milltail Creek, and it empties into the Alligator River some eight or ten miles south of the present town of East Lake and only a few miles from the recently completed Lindsay Warren Bridge.

This capital of the Matchapungos was almost inacces-sible except by navigating the creek from its delta, and thus the settlement was in a strategically strong defen-sive location. The village itself was built on what is called a "hammock"—a sort of broad plateau of high, fertile land completely surrounded by swamp, marsh, or bog. On these elevated acres the Indians raised crops of corn and a wheatlike grain as well as highly cultivated grapes and a variety of tobaccos. Here the medicine man had his herb garden, and here the abundant chinquapin trees and nutoaks were protected and used as sources of food. The creek held countless delicious mussels which some-times yielded the pearls so treasured by these simple people. The surrounding territory was rich in wild game. Turkey, bear, rabbit, deer, quail, and dove abounded; and the waters of the nearby sounds and rivers teemed with fish. The entire area is now known as "Beechland," and the majority of it is owned by the West Virginia Pulp and Paper Company.

Within the memory of men still living there was at Beechland a tribe of fair-haired, blue-eyed Indians. Some of these people still bear the names of colonists who were carried on Governor White's rolls as having been left on Roanoke. These unusual people have such names as John White, Culbert White, John Bright, Thomas Coleman, Richard Taverner, John Gibbs, James Hynde, Michael Bishop, Thomas Phevens, and last but by no means least, Henry Paine. Of course, it may be just co-incidence that these names are exactly the names of some of the missing colonists.

Old-timers also tell us that this Indian settlement was peculiar in another way. Many of the houses are said to have been two-story houses, a type of construction unknown to Indians elsewhere. Further, these houses had thatched roofs, not coverings of skin, and were constructed of riven boards, not timbers chopped or burned in the Indian fashion. The stairways leading to the second stories of these ancient houses were not ladder-like but were stairs also built of riven boards and supported by risers. Among the traditions of these Matchapungo Indians are persistent stories of ancestors who could "talk out of a book"—an obvious reference, it seems, to reading from a book. Coincidence? Ask Thomas Mann of Mann's Harbor. There's no doubt in that honest man's mind. He's lived a long and honorable life in that area, and he verily believes that the colony was not "lost" at all but still lives in the descendants of those English and Indian allies who fled Roanoke Island together.

A few years ago when the West Virginia Pulp and Paper Company was doing some excavating for timbering purposes, they had to dig into a rather large mound near Beechland. In this mound, in the heart of the wilderness, they found numerous Indian artifacts, arrowheads, works of pottery, and potsherds. They also found several riven coffins which were made from solid cypress wood. They were made in a form that can be best described as two canoes—one canoe being the top half of the coffin, and the other the bottom half. On the top of each of these coffins was plainly and deeply chiseled a Roman or Latin cross, the type that has come to be universally and traditionally accepted as the cross of Christianity. Beneath each cross were the unmistakable letters, *I N R I.* These are thought to represent the traditional "Jesus Nazarenus, Rex Judaeorum" or, translated, "Jesus of Nazareth, King of the Jews," the inscription which adorned the cross of Christ at the time of the crucifixion. It was common practice in Elizabethan times to write the letter "I" for the letter "J." It was simpler and was accepted by the literate people of that day. A riven coffin with English carvings buried in the midst of a wilderness in an Indian burial ground—is that coincidence?

In the center of this plateau at Beechland there is an extensive field, which the forest has not retaken and which has been known through the centuries as the "Malocki Old Indian Field." This field at one time, before the American Revolution, is said to have been owned by an Indian named Malocki Paine, son of one Henry Paine. It seems obvious that the name "Malocki" is an Indian corruption of the old Biblical name Malachi. If you should ask one of the older residents of this area if he knows of the Malocki Old Indian Field, he will tell you that he does and will identify it for you. If you ask about the Malachi Indian Field, it rings no bell with him whatsoever.

This Malocki Paine was a very real flesh-and-blood person. He too was blond-haired and blue-eyed, as was his lovely sister. His sister was one of the ancestors of the Honorable Frank Cahoon, Sheriff of Dare County. Frank is very proud of that fact, and well has he the right to be. He is not one to brag about anything, but you can see the quiet pride in him when his ancestor is discussed. Ask him if he is sensitive about the possibility that he is descended from one of the survivors of the so-called Lost Colony, and he will tell you that he is proud that such a possibility exists. "I consider the Matchapungo Indians to be the real original settlers of this territory, and I am extremely proud of the part they took in helping Sir Walter Raleigh's Lost Colony."

This, then, is the evidence as it has been gathered to the time of this writing. Someday interested historians and antiquarians are going to dig, literally, deeper into Beechland. What they find may well bring a thrill just as great as, and much more personal than, the finding of the tomb of Pharoah Tutankhamen. At least, I shall feel that it is more personal for me.

Now, Beechland is under lease to the United States Navy and Air Force. It is being used as a practice bombing range for the planes of both services. Admission is gained only by invitation and is supervised by the Navy and the Air Force. The area is as dangerous to the unwary visitor today as it was in the time of Chief Manteo. You could step off one of those dirt roads and never be seen again. Bear are still there, rattlesnakes almost as big as a man's thigh, as well as an assortment of wildcats. The practice bombs are supposed to be nonexplosive, but you could get yourself killed with a minimum of effort in that section.

Until the location is made available for excavation and further study by competent and professional anthropologists, history once again with an enigmatic smile must draw the veil and leave us to weigh the evidence we have.

Anyway, I like to think that old Henry Paine and Malocki Paine and even Eleanor Dare herself are proud to know that their land is contributing to the welfare and the excellence of those armed forces who are keeping their weapons sharp for the defense of liberty in this land to which they came. Rest well, you pioneer patriots! Your torch of liberty still burns brightly in this cradle of civilization which you founded in the wilderness nearly four hundred years ago. We shall keep your faith.

4
JOCKEY'S RIDGE AND NAG'S HEAD

Called "the largest sand hill on the Atlantic coast," a veritable sand mountain looms on Nag's Head beach between mileposts twelve and thirteen, just north of the now-paved road running from the ocean side to the old Sound side. Even a casual observer cannot help being impressed by the bulk of this enormous pile of sand made up of two interlocking ridges. The fascination of the observer with this natural wonder is made even more complete when he learns that this very spot has been the scene both of romance and of sheer, stark terror.

This tremendous dune has been known since time immemorial as "Jockey's Ridge." Not Jockey Ridge, but Jockey's Ridge. Few things can rouse the ire of an old Nag's Header quicker than the omission of that apostrophe-*s* from the name of this beloved landmark upon which some of the most distinguished troths in North Carolina have been plighted and upon whose broad bosom many a Governor and Supreme Court Justice has, as a child, made merry at a wiener roast or marshmallow toast.

Long before the days of paved roads and electricity

and indoor plumbing on the Outer Banks, even before the "original thirteen" cottages of the "unpainted aristocracy" were built, there lived at what is now known as Nag's Head a hardy, independent tribe of fishermen and hunters who wrested a living, year-round, from the ocean, the sounds, the marshes, and the woods. No pirates were these, but honest and God-fearing outdoorsmen, horny of hand and clear of conscience, whose wants were few and whose pleasures were simple and robust.

Occupying the same general territory at the same time was an equally hardy and independent tribe of wild marsh ponies, the descendants of survivors from shipwrecks, who asked nothing from man but to be let alone.

This, of course, man refused to do. Inevitably some of these fine animals were chased into the ocean shallows or hemmed up in the woods and captured. The blood of some of the finest Arabian stallions is said to have run in the veins of these swift and strong little horses, and to own one was the source of much quiet pride. It was only natural that rivalries should grow up between villages and between individuals as to whose horse was the faster. Challenge races soon became common, and it was not long before tracks or paths were laid out and rules adopted for the conduct of these races.

One of the most popular of these tracks was located on the flat, hard surface of the sand that lay to the south and west of the great sand mountain at Nag's Head beach. Not only was the terrain there nearly ideal for horse racing, but the steep sides of the dune made an ideal grandstand which could have held thousands of people. Indeed, it did hold nearly the entire population

of Nag's Head, Collington, Kitty Hawk, and other more outlying settlements whenever horse racing was scheduled.

This, then, is the origin of the name of Jockey's Ridge. It was the logical designation for this natural grandstand and serves today as an appropriate monument to the ingenuity of those early Bankers. Having little in the way of entertainment at hand, they made their own entertainment and, in so doing, took full advantage of all that nature offered in the way of facilities.

The wild horses and marsh ponies are just about all gone now. There are a few left on Ocracoke Island and other scattered islands along the coast, but this is all that is left of the once large herds which ran as wild and free as the foxes on the beaches. It was a never-to-be-forgotten experience and a sight of matchless beauty on a moonlit night to lie perfectly still, almost without breathing, concealed by a clump of sea oats and to watch the leader of a wild herd come cautiously down upon the beach, scout the area carefully, and then proceed with his forefeet to paw a hole in the sand until fresh water was reached. Once the water was found and tested, the little stallion would stand back and resume his guard duty while his little mares would come and drink from the hole he had provided. Perceiving a sudden noise or movement—maybe only the scurrying of a sandfiddler—they would vanish into the dunes in an instant with tossing manes and the Lilliputian thunder of tiny hooves.

I never attended a "pony-penning," as some of the roundups were called. I did not want to see these beautiful, wild things deprived of their liberty. I preferred, and I still prefer, to remember the tiny stallion, wild and free as God made him, every sense alert and every muscle taut on that moonlit beach as he stood watch over his harem. He, too, was a genuine Outer Banker.

Many years before these happy, golden days, however, this then-lonely but wildly beautiful locale had quite a different flavor. What stories of abject horror these sands could tell! What wild tales of murder and robbery could this sand mountain relate, if one had ears to listen. Whispers and vignettes of this wild and savage past come to us in the very name of the beach itself.

Quite possibly you have heard that this portion of the Outer Banks of North Carolina, which is called by the unusual name of Nag's Head, was named after some pirate-frequented beach on the coast of England near Penzance. There was such an English beach which bore such a name. You may have been told, on the other hand, that some ancient cartographer of the Governor John White era fancied he saw some resemblance in the shape of the Carolina coast to the outline of a horse's head, and thus evolved the name. This is an interesting speculation, but it is quite certain that no such name appears on any of Governor White's maps or in the sketches of Amadas and Barlowe, Ralph Lane, or any of the other explorers of that day.

The descendants of the early settlers of this region tell an entirely different story, and the sometimes bloody chapters in the history of this storied land certainly seem to bear them out. This is the true account according to those who should know.

By the late sixteen hundreds the Outer Banks (Portsmouth Island, Ocracoke Island, Hatteras Island, and Nag's Head) had already acquired a sparse population.

This was composed partly of castaways from various wrecks that had either come ashore or had foundered off this treacherous coast. These castaways were for the most part sailors, men who had followed the sea from childhood and who were poorly equipped to do anything else. Having only by the barest of margins escaped death by drowning, most of them had had quite enough of a sailor's life and had turned to, trying to make a living ashore. Here they ran into one of the bitterly hard facts of life on the Outer Banks of that day. There was practically no livelihood except fishing. Not only was fishing hard and dangerous work, but it was sometimes unproductive work as well.

Present among these shipwrecked mariners were a goodly number of men who, at one time or another, had been part of the crews of pirate ships. Some of them had drifted into piracy by joining the crews of privateers licensed by the government to prey upon enemy shipping. Because of the slowness of the communications of the day, it was not unheard of that these mariners, uninformed of the ending of official hostilities, should continue their privateering even after peace had been negotiated. Thus they became *de-facto* pirates, afraid to return home for fear of the consequences. Edward Drummond of England, later known as Edward Teach or Blackbeard, started his nautical life as a self-respecting privateersman under the command of a Captain Hornigold. When his commander "took the pledge and went ashore," Teach took over one of Hornigold's ships and became one of the most dreaded pirates ever to sail American coastal waters. He had a large home on Ocracoke Island.

These shipwrecked pirates were men of the same general stripe. They had no scruples whatsoever about turning an easy doubloon by force of arms, nor were they physical cowards. It is not surprising that some of the bolder and more evil of them should have conspired together to find a way to reap the sometimes rich hauls of piracy, while at the same time remaining snug ashore in this land that had given them haven from the sea.

Alexander Hamilton had known and feared this treacherous coast as a boy, and it was at his insistence that the first lighthouse at Cape Hatteras had been erected to warn ships offshore of the dangerous reefs of that stormy cape. Farther north there were no lighthouses at that time. The Carolina coast was totally unlighted from Hatteras all the way to Virginia. Hamilton had wanted several warning beacons erected but had settled for this light at the most dangerous point of all. It was on the unmarked and unlighted section that our land pirates found the locale they were seeking.

Thus by a combination of circumstance, cupidity, and cunning, there was created a highly organized band of land pirates, a brotherhood of the sea gone ashore. This is how they operated. Knowing from their bitter personal experience the scarcity of navigational aids, such as lighthouses, buoys, bells, and whistles, they conceived a diabolical plan for luring unsuspecting ships ashore to make them pile up on the beach that they might be the more easily boarded and looted.

To carry out their plan, they would choose a dark and starless night on which a ship offshore would find it virtually impossible to determine her exact position. On such a night these brigands would lead an old nag to the top of Jockey's Ridge and affix a stave securely to one of the front legs of the animal. The nag, limping along the crest of the ridge, would proceed with its head bobbing in a slow and irregular series of gentle curves up and down. To the head of this hobbled nag they would affix a ship's running light, of which there were plenty to be had from the numerous wrecks along the shore. A green running light would be used for starboard; a red, for larboard—depending on whether they intended to lead the nag north or south.

Thus, as the nag was led along the top of the ridge, it appeared to ship captains offshore that yonder a short distance to the west was a vessel either making slow progress or else riding at anchor in an apparently peaceful sea. This was reason enough for them to alter course and to try to hail the supposed vessel to determine position and to exchange mail and news. Such was common practice, at the time, if two ships passed within hailing distance of each other, even if there was no doubt about position.

By the time the unsuspecting captain had sailed his ship into the breakers, it was too late to alter course again. In fact, it was too late to do anything at all except to put up the best fight possible. Caught between the relentless sea pounding on one side and the shoals and reefs threatening on the other, and with a terrifying horde of pirates armed with swords and pistols swarming up over the sides from small boats, the jig was indeed up.

Small wonder it is that not one ship lured ashore ever escaped capture and complete destruction by these land pirates of Nag's Head. The crew and any passengers were summarily killed, and none were ever known to have escaped.

None, that is, with the exception of one very lovely young lady. But that is another story, which must await its place in another part of this volume.

5
THE PIRATE LIGHTS OF PAMLICO SOUND

Ocracoke and Portsmouth islands are permeated with the ghost of Blackbeard, most famous of all American pirates. There is scarcely a beach on either Sound or ocean shore of these islands that has not echoed to the booming roar of his voice and felt the heavy tread of his tremendous boots. Ocracoke was his village, and he loved it with a fierce and jealous affection, which he obviously did not feel for Hatteras, although he frequently visited that island as well. It was on Ocracoke that this famous brigand lived, drank his rum, and roared his threats against British authority. Bath Town was another home he loved, but it was not near the sea, his natural habitat.

Blackbeard had good cause, he thought, to defy British authority. He was often heard to complain in a most profane manner about a king who would train an honest seaman in a way of life and then turn about and make it a crime to live that way of life. Born in Bristol, England, and christened Edward Drummond, he went to sea at an early age as a cabin boy. As a young man he served as a seaman aboard a British privateer in what is known to history as Queen Anne's War. Under this arrangement it was perfectly legal for, and the patriotic duty of, the captain of a ship licensed as a privateer to attack a merchant ship flying the flag of France, impress or imprison the merchantman's crew, and then share in the division of the captured ship's cargo. Of course, sometimes a Spanish flag was mistaken for a French one, but the wartime government of Britain was not inclined to quibble over technicalities. Under this arrangement the crown was spared the expense of paying the crew and of outfitting and supplying the ship, enemy shipping was destroyed or captured, and a portion of valuable cargoes was delivered to the official treasury. All that was necessary was a license as a privateer, and a captain became his own naval commander, his own tactician, and his own bookkeeper for the division of spoils. Some of the very best and bravest of English captains served at one time or another as privateers. The profits were huge.

When the war had come to an end, though, and peace was made with France, what had been patriotism became piracy; and this was the burden of Blackbeard's complaint—or at least so he said! At the war's end Edward Teach (he had changed his name from Drummond to Teach or Thatch or Tatch) was a lieutenant under a Captain Hornigold, a very successful privateer. The crown offered amnesty to all former privateersmen and/or pirates who would reform and swear an oath of law-abiding fealty to the king and, of course, surrender to the crown such captured ships as they were using.

Captain Hornigold decided to take the king's pardon. He moved ashore, took the oath, and settled down to enjoy the profits of his former occupation. Since Teach, however, had no accumulated wealth, he just kept possession of the ship that Hornigold had given him to command and set sail for the Americas to seek his own fortune. If there had been any doubt before, that act branded Edward Teach a pirate.

Renaming his vessel the *Queen Anne's Revenge* and recruiting as desperate and able a crew from the "brotherhood of the sea" as can well be imagined, he soon made a name for himself as the scourge of the Atlantic seaboard. He even took on the British man-of-war H.M.S. *Scarborough* and fought her on even terms for several hours before the *Scarborough* broke off the engagement and ran for cover. It was after this victory that Teach adopted the name "Blackbeard."

He was the possessor of a magnificent, bushy beard the color of jet. This hirsute adornment extended from just beneath his eyes all the way down to his waist, hiding his belt buckle. It was almost as wide as his barrel-shaped chest and served as a sort of banner or rallying flag for his henchmen in the thick of hand-to-hand battle. Since Teach was nearly seven feet in height, this expanse of beard was awe-inspiring to friend and foe alike. To make his appearance even more frightful, he would twist little pigtails in his beard and tie them with red ribbons. Then he would coil a snakelike, slow-burning match of punk around his head just over his ears and under the brim of his hat. When both ends of this decoration were lit and smoking and his white teeth were gleaming in an evil grin amidst that heavy black beard, our pirate might well have been mistaken for the devil himself.

Completely fearless, this giant of a pirate roamed the Atlantic at will, taking as he went prizes in the form of noble ships, which he either sunk or else manned with a prize crew of pirates. Never one to hang back from the thick of personal combat, Blackbeard always led the charge of the fearsome boarding parties that swarmed from the deck of the *Revenge* onto the scuppers of the victim. The sight of this monster with what looked like blazing horns protruding from his brow, red ribbons bedecking a huge beard, a pistol in one hand and a gleaming sword in the other, was enough to frighten any defender half to death to begin with. Even the mention of his name was enough to strike fear into the hearts of merchants and seamen alike. At one time he actually blockaded the City of Charleston, South Carolina, with his one ship and forced that proud city to pay a ransom of a fortune in drugs and medicines before he sailed away, keeping his word not to put the city to the torch once the ransom was paid.

Blackbeard's favorite territory, though, seemed to be Ocracoke and Portsmouth. He could sell his captured cargoes to the merchants there much cheaper than they could buy elsewhere and without their having to pay a farthing of British tariff. This was the territory that he considered to be his home base. Here he went to careen his ships, repair battle damage, and fit them out for more piracy. On Ocracoke Island he built himself a large and comfortable house. Two stories high and containing many large rooms, this house became known through the years as "Blackbeard's Castle." This is where the pirate lived when he came ashore and where he counted and arranged his treasure before moving it to hiding places which, according to his own statement shortly before his death, were known only to the devil and to the pirate captain himself. Blackbeard's large castle was abandoned after his death to grow up in weeds and was almost completely hidden by the undergrowth. It was finally torn down in the name of "progress" to make way for a more modern structure.

It was near Ocracoke Inlet that an incident took place which resulted in the permanent crippling of Israel Hands, first mate of the pirate band. It seems that Teach and Hands were sitting at a table with a third brigand drinking rum. They were below decks in their ship, and a single candle on the table gave a faint light to the scene. In a "test of courage" Blackbeard pulled his loaded pistol from his belt and held it under the table. Vowing to shoot any man who did not run, he then blew out the candle and started counting. The crewman broke and ran, but Israel Hands remained sitting and continued to drink from his goblet. With no compunction whatsoever, Blackbeard pulled the trigger and blasted away in the direction of the chair in which he had last seen his trusted mate before blowing out the candle. The slug hit the unlucky Israel in the knee and ranged upward into his thigh. Rum was administered, and the bullet was cut out of his leg then and there, but Israel Hands remained crippled from that wound as long as he lived. This rugged pirate was the prototype from which Robert Louis Stevenson created his fictional pirate of the story *Treasure Island*. Stevenson even gave his creation the name of this first mate of the Blackbeard ship.

Present-day charts of the waters around Ocracoke still show "Teach's Hole," where the drunken master pirate's aim in the darkness was still accurate enough to cripple his good friend.

At one time in his career Blackbeard apparently decided to give up piracy. He had amassed a goodly amount of treasure to live on, and he got the idea that he would like to live ashore. Sailing into Bath Town, he notified the British authorities that he was reformed, that he wished to mend his evil ways and take the oath of loyalty to the crown. Full pardon was granted to "our newly loyal subject" by the authorities, and he gave up his ship and bought a house on the point of Bath Creek. He even married the sixteen-year-old daughter of a local farmer and made her mistress of his home. What, if anything, he did about wives he was reputed to have in Elizabeth City, in Edenton, and in Ocracoke is unknown, but it is unlikely the four ladies ever met one another.

A "gentleman's life ashore" apparently meant one long drunken spree for our hero, for that is exactly how he lived it. Shamefully mistreating his young wife and opening his house and his purse to any and all comers, he dissipated in a short time the tidy fortune he had brought ashore. Then, too, he began to have a genuine hunger for the sea and for shipboard life. He was a child of the sea, and he never felt really at home unless he was walking the deck of an ocean-going vessel. At length he bought and fitted out such a boat and told all and sundry she was to be used as an honest seagoing merchantman. Naming his new craft the *Adventure*, he never did explain the meaning of the gun-ports along both her sides, shutters that swung open to reveal the ugly snouts of cannon mounted 'tween decks.

Off to sea sailed the *Adventure* with Edward Teach as her skipper, and back she came, time after time, towing crewless ships that Teach claimed to have found abandoned on the open sea with cargoes untouched. He still insisted that he was an honest merchant seaman who had had the extreme good luck to find his prizes floating derelict on the ocean. Once again his fortunes began to rise.

After a few months of this pretense, Blackbeard tired of the sham and openly returned to pirating. That way he didn't have to kill all the captured crews, and many of them came to be valued crewmen in his raider. With complete impartiality, our pirate preyed on the shipping of all nations. He would as soon sink a British ship as a Spanish one, nor was the commerce of the American merchants safe from his depredations.

Then Edward Teach's overleaping ambition proved his undoing. Not content with the fruit of his own labors, he conceived the grandiose scheme of fortifying Ocracoke Island and making it into a haven and refuge for all pirate ships. He himself was to reign there as a sort of king of the pirates while they were in his stronghold. As a fee for such sanctuary, he planned to charge each incoming ship a percentage of the prize money for the privilege of membership in the club.

This plan would probably have succeeded, because Teach was a master strategist and would have had capable help. The ship owners and merchants of the Carolinas heard of this dream, however, and were appalled at the prospect. Despairing of any help whatsoever from

Governor Eden in Bath, they sent a delegation to Governor Spotswood of the colony of Virginia, imploring his aid and that of the British navy. Spotswood agreed to help and promised to send a raiding party composed of men from two British warships then in Virginia ports.

And so it came about that, in November, 1718, Blackbeard was at anchor in his ship *Adventure* outside the peaceful harbor at Ocracoke near the spot called Blackbeard's or Teach's Hole. He was expecting no trouble, but he had his full crew aboard, and the *Adventure* was repaired and in good shape for the sea.

Unknown to the pirates, two sloops under the command of a Lieutenant Maynard had arrived late the night before. Sent, as promised by Governor Spotswood, to search for the pirates, these ships were manned by British sailors and marines from the British navy. They were under orders to take the brigand Blackbeard dead or alive. This they intended to do.

At dawn on that clear, cold November day, Lieutenant Maynard sent out two small skiffs to take soundings to try to find the depth of the water near the anchored *Adventure*. If possible, they were to find a deep-water access to the pirate craft. These strange and suspicious-looking craft were fired on by the *Adventure* when they failed to answer a hail. The accurate small-arms fire from the *Adventure* was intended to warn rather than to harm, but it drove the skiffs back to their parent ship in a hurry.

At this point, the British ensign was run up on both sloops, and Blackbeard's hail was answered by a volley of rifle fire as the smaller of the two sloops set her sails and tried to find a channel through the sand bars to engage the *Adventure*. The channel was as tricky then as it is now, and the Britisher ran hard aground and stuck fast. This greatly delighted Teach, who knew these waters as most men know their dooryards. This stranded smaller sloop would be easy prey after he had dealt with the larger vessel, he thought.

That larger sloop, the *Ranger*, was under the personal command of Maynard, who immediately got her under way and sailed closer to Blackbeard to make his small-arms fire more effective. To Blackbeard's great glee, the *Ranger* also ran aground, but what appeared to be a more-or-less permanent stranding turned out in a few moments to have been only a temporary disabling of Maynard's vessel. Thinking he now had the *Ranger* at his mercy, Blackbeard slipped his anchor cable and left the secure position he had held behind the sand reef. Under a favorable wind and keeping to the familiar channel, he ran straight for the *Ranger*.

At Teach's bellowed order, the gun-ports were opened on both sides of the *Adventure*, and the cannon were run out, so that their muzzles protruded beyond the sides of the ship. Charges and load were placed in each cannon, and matches were made ready. Down bore the pirate ship upon the *Ranger*. At the last moment before collision, she turned alongside and brought her starboard guns to bear. The cannon fired almost as one, raking the *Ranger* fore and aft. As the *Adventure* then wheeled to return and present her larboard battery, Maynard hastily ordered his men below decks. Around came the buccaneer and sailed smartly back. This time the larboard cannon fired, again sweeping the decks of the *Ranger* fore and aft. However, this time there were no casualties since only the dead from the previous salvo had remained on deck with Maynard.

Seeing an apparently helpless sloop at his mercy, Teach then gave the order to come alongside and board the *Ranger*. Even as the grappling irons were being thrown, however, Maynard called to his men below decks, and they swarmed back topside, armed to the teeth with pistols and swords.

As was his custom, Teach led the screaming, howling charge of men from one craft to the other. Cutlass and pistol in hand, he sprang to the deck of the *Ranger* and immediately sought out her commanding officer. For one brief instant in eternity Blackbeard and Maynard glared into each other's eyes. Then, with a curse, Blackbeard charged, only to be met by the pointblank fire from Maynard's pistol. Tearing a groove along the side of the pirate's head, the bullet crazed but did not kill him. With a roar of pain and anger, Teach sprang once again for his adversary; but this time one of Maynard's sword-wielding marines attacked him from the side. Swinging the heavy blade down with both hands and with all his might, the marine cut so deeply into the side of Blackbeard's neck that it seemed he almost severed the great head from its body.

With blood spouting from this gigantic cut and gore from his head wound almost blinding him, our pirate, nonetheless, closed with Maynard in an attempt to kill him as, all around them, the boarding party fought desperately with the Britishers. Maynard was too skillful a swordsman to be pinned down, and he fenced with Blackbeard, eluding him, dodging, and inflicting yet more wounds on the huge body. The magnificent beard was now covered with matted blood, and the cruel eyes were beginning to glaze. Finally, Teach drew back one step, raised his pistol with his left hand to blast his enemy, and fell forward on his face, quite dead, the smouldering match still around his head and almost touching the boots of Lieutenant Maynard. When they examined the body later, it was found that Teach had sustained some thirty-seven major wounds, including that deadly cut in his neck, any one of which would have stopped a lesser man.

Seeing their leader fall, the pirates then jumped into Pamlico Sound and swam or waded ashore. Their liberty was short lived, however, since they were all rounded up and taken back to Virginia for trial. All but Israel Hands and one other were convicted of piracy and treason and were hanged. Hands turned state's evidence and escaped the death penalty.

When Blackbeard had been killed, his head was cut off and affixed to the bowsprit of the *Ranger*. There it remained until the ship returned to Virginia. What was finally done with the grisly trophy is not recorded, but there is one fine family in Massachusetts which claims that the skull was made into a giant cup, was then silver-plated, and is now in their possession. The great, mutilated body of Blackbeard was tossed unceremoniously overboard where, legend claims, it swam three times around the entangled *Ranger* and *Adventure* before it sank from sight beneath the water.

Israel Hands, Blackbeard's crippled first mate, returned to England after the piracy trial and lived out his life in London. Governor Spotswood, however, although his term as Governor had expired, steadfastly refused to return to England. He gave as his reason his fear of what other pirates might do to him—the man who had been responsible for the death of the famous Blackbeard—if they could manage to capture him. Thus did the fear generated by Blackbeard actually outlive the man himself.

Many men have tried to discover the fabled treasure that Blackbeard admitted having buried. Legend has it that Teach traveled as far inland as the site of the present town of Grimesland, some ten miles east of Greenville, North Carolina, on the Tar River. At this location the pirate is said to have had a sister, who lived on a small farm which he had bought for her and which, in fact, still bears her name in the ancient records of the county. Blackbeard is said to have visited her on several occasions to recuperate from wounds and from extended sprees. There is an extremely old cypress tree near this site. With its roots in the waters of the river, it towers above all the other trees in the area. This tree is called "Old Table-Top" and was used as a lookout where the brigand stationed one of his henchmen to keep watch down the river and to warn against sudden attack. The tree is, indeed, flat across the top, and it would be a comparatively easy matter to construct a platform there which would command a view of Tar River almost to the town of Washington. Great excitement prevailed in that neighborhood in 1933 when a Mr. Lee dug out of the river bank nearby a small iron pot half-filled with old silver coins of various sizes.

Blount's Creek near Washington, North Carolina, is another location where the treasure has been hunted and dug for, as well as Holliday's Island near the town of

Edenton. If any of the searchers found any treasure, they have kept the secret well. A farmer did plow up a metal bucket near Bath and found therein a number of silver coins and three gold coins, all of foreign make and all very old, but these were never definitely tied to Teach, and it is thought that perhaps some settler fearful of an Indian attack buried them there.

To this day at Ocracoke some will tell you that the "Teach lights" are still seen on occasion both over and in the waters of Pamlico Sound. Blackbeard's ghostly ship is sometimes seen in the light of the waning moon. Some say the headless figure of Blackbeard can be seen in the dark of the moon as it swims around and around Teach's Hole, searching for its severed head. They aver that it gleams with a phosphorescent glow and is plainly visible just below the surface of the water.

When Teach's lights are seen, either above or below the surface of the water, it always portends disaster of some sort for the ones who see them. If there be a man brave or foolish enough to follow those lights until they come to rest, he would find Blackbeard's buried treasure. The only trouble is, he would also find the devil himself, sitting cross-legged on the treasure and claiming his half as Blackbeard's sworn partner.

6
OLD QUORK

Nearly everything is motorized today. With the speed and comparative ease of automotive transportation one tends, if one is not careful, to whiz past some of the most fascinating legends of our past.

For instance, as you pass swiftly southward today over the paved roads that link Kitty Hawk to Kill Devil Hills to Nag's Head and soar up and over storied Oregon Inlet on the magnificent Bonner Bridge and onward past Pea Island to Hatteras Island, it is not even necessary to slacken your speed before you reach Hatteras Inlet itself, where the pavement stops at the ferry slip.

Even the ferry trip is a short and easy one, and you roll ashore on the northern end of Ocracoke Island with only some thirteen miles remaining between you and Ocracoke Village itself. Nearly every one of those thirteen miles has its own legend, and you are now truly traversing fabulous territory.

If you slow your pace now and look sharply, you will notice by the side of the highway an official sign of the North Carolina Highway Department bearing the words: "Old Quork Point." As is the case with most of the place names on these Outer Banks, thereby hangs a tale—a legend that many of the inhabitants will assure you is quite true.

It is well known and clearly remembered here that "Old Quork" was the name of a man, a castaway, who, like so many others, had washed up on Ocracoke Island the survivor of a shipwreck and had elected to remain there among the friendly and courageous people who had helped him to survive. This Old Quork was apparently a person of Arabian origin. His skin is said to have been of a sort of light gold color, and his name such an outlandish mixture of contradictory and guttural sounds that the nearest the native tongue could come to pronouncing it was to mimic the sound the croaker fish makes. So "Quork" he became, and this was soon lengthened to *Old* Quork because of his strange and outlandish habits and mannerisms. Thus he was known for the rest of his natural life.

This newly arrived citizen soon developed into a mighty fisherman. He quickly learned the skills and the methods the Islanders had developed for making their living from the ocean. They were generously willing to teach, and he was avidly eager to learn. It was not long before he owned his own boat, having made a sharp trade with the widow of a fisherman who had died ashore of an undiagnosed ailment at the ripe old age of 94. The boat was almost as old as her former owner, but she was soundly built and was both seaworthy and seakindly.

Old Quork was quick of hand and as sure-footed as a cat. So far as could be told, he was not afraid of anything that walked, crawled, or swam. That part of his make-up the Bankers could understand and appreciate, but there were other facets of his personality of which they were dubious. As a matter of fact, there were some who, even then, were vaguely suspicious of Quork's extraordinary good luck with a net. There were those who wondered out loud just why the sharks never got into his nets and tore them, why the trash fish seemed to avoid his seine, and how it was that he seemed able to make better hauls singlehandedly than other boats could make even by working together.

The thing, however, that disturbed his fellow fishermen most was the fact that Old Quork had no religious feelings whatsoever. His complete lack of any sense of reverence for an almighty power shocked and outraged these people who had in their time known and respected Moslems, Buddhists, and Hindus—all reduced to the common denominator of castaways but all holding to their own particular kind of belief in an omnipotent deity.

And so it transpired that on the morning of February 6, 1788, just one month to the day after Old Christmas had been celebrated (and it is still celebrated in the village of Rodanthe on Hatteras Island), Old Quork put out in his fishing boat from a point of land near Ocracoke Village. He had his nets in order and neatly folded in the stern of his boat. His sails were spread to the freshening wind, which the old-timers had predicted would ripen into a full gale before the next high tide. As always, he sailed alone, and it was not long before his boat disappeared over the horizon.

As the day wore on, and the weather worsened, fears

were felt for Quork, and some concern was expressed for his safety. He was a queer one, all right, but none could deny that he was a brave and able fisherman, and the Ocracokers certainly did not wish him any harm. It was with some sense of relief, then, that they spied his boat headed again for the shore. She seemed low in the water, and she seemed to be making unusually heavy weather of it, but she was traveling at a goodly speed, and soon Quork brought her through the inlet and into the calmer waters of Pamlico Sound. As he tied up at the public dock, the reason for the boat's trim became apparent. She was literally loaded to the gunwales with various sorts and sizes of good, marketable fish.

Rejoicing in Quork's continued good luck, his neighbors helped him unload his catch. Seldom had they seen such a harvest of good fish. There were trout, flounder, bluefish, and mullet. There were spot, croaker, redfish, and drum, but not a single trash fish in the lot. When they were loaded onto the shore end of the dock, they made a great pile. You could almost see the wheels turning in Quork's head as he tried to compute his profit on this one haul.

By now the wind had quickened into a half-gale, and the breakers at sea were growing larger and larger. They were also commencing the familiar roar that characterizes some of the winter storms in this area. The fishermen were congratulating themselves upon getting Quork's boat unloaded before the Sound became too rough for such work, when what did they behold to their surprise but Quork himself refolding his nets, refilling his drinking-water jugs, and obviously preparing his sails for a return to the worsening sea.

Noticing the wild light in his eyes, they tried to persuade Old Quork that it was foolhardy to risk a return trip to sea in the face of such weather. Strongly did they remonstrate with him and, overlooking his past coolness to them, begged and pleaded with him, pointing out that the sea was already too rough, that it was bound to get much worse rather than better, and that it would be flying in the face of the Almighty Himself to put out needlessly in such weather.

According to the legend, Old Quork responded with a scornful laugh and continued his preparations. Finally, all being ready aboard his ancient craft, Old Quork, it is said, stood up in the stern sheets of his boat and, fully aware of his audience on the wharf, shook his fist at the threatening heavens, and defied God. "If there is a God up there, show Yourself now," roared Old Quork. "I, Old Quork, am a greater god than any so-called Heavenly Father; and by the devil and with Satan's help and protection, I will put out to my fishing grounds, and I will come back with an even bigger catch before this day is done!" Then, with a flourish, Quork cast off his mooring lines, hoisted his mainsail, and, with lee gunwale almost awash, conned his small boat toward the wild waters of the inlet.

Aghast, his neighbors watched as he successfully and almost miraculously traversed the inlet and reached the open sea. So far, his fantastic luck was holding. Amazed, the watchers saw him alter his course and trim his sails as he headed his wildly bucking and pitching vessel into the very eye of the worsening storm.

Some say that just before he sailed out of sight—a lone figure in the driving rain and spume—they heard a high,

mocking laugh that carried to the watchers on the shore even above the roar of the wind. Others declare that it sounded to them more like the scream of a human in mortal terror.

Be that as it may, Old Quork was never seen again, dead or alive. Nor was any fragment of his boat or his nets ever found. On all of Ocracoke Island there was only the great pile of fish to show that he had ever lived there. That pile of fish stayed right there, too, until it got so ripe it had to be shoveled into the Sound to make a feast for the crabs.

This is the story of Old Quork. This is the man the point was named for. And if you wonder if Ocracokers really believe this yarn, just try to get certain ones of them to go fishing on February 6, any year. You will not be able to force or bribe them even to set foot in a boat, much less to venture out on the water. Of course, some of the young ones will, but they get dark and forbidding looks from their elders. "Old Quork Day" is a day remembered in their folklore with apprehension and fear.

The name you read on the highway sign as you approach Ocracoke Village marks the very point from which Old Quork is said to have sailed out in his boat. They call it Old Quork's Point, and if you decide to try a little flounder gigging on that point some February 6 —and if you get back—drop me a line and let me know how you came out.

7
THE SEVEN SISTERS

In the days before that conflict now called the War Between the States, Nag's Head on the Outer Banks was a very fashionable and popular summer resort for the gentry of eastern North Carolina. A few people went farther north to a place called Willoughby Spit, and some traveled down to Wilmington and Southport. Most of the summerlong vacationers, however, went to Nag's Head.

Whole families would come either on a chartered boat or by private sailing vessel. They would bring with them their dogs, their cats, horses, cows, pigs, flocks of chickens, and all their own and most of their neighbors' children as well. Thus supplied, as though they were a colonizing expedition, they would set up housekeeping for the entire summer. At least one cook and her husband would accompany each family, and these housekeepers usually made a little colony of their own.

At Nag's Head itself about opposite milepost fourteen, the present-day visitor will observe some seven contiguous hills of sand of nearly equal size and beauty. These lie between the paved bypass and Roanoke Sound.

They form a chain and are known as "the Seven Sisters." As is the case with most place names on the Outer Banks, this name has a meaning and significance based on actual events that occurred long ago.

Sometime after the American Revolution but many years before the War Between the States, there lived in Perquimans County near the colonial settlement of Durant's Neck a landed gentleman by the name of Thomas Nixon, Esq. This gentleman is the ancestor of the Thomas Nixon who was the father of Marjorie Nixon Oakey and Dorothy Nixon Horton, prominent citizens of Hertford, and of Edna Jones Nixon Dawson, wife of the Coca-Cola magnate of Washington, North Carolina.

This ante-bellum Mr. Nixon was a man of considerable property in Perquimans County, owning not only a great deal of land but also many slaves. Local tradition has it that he was a very kind and humane master, who took a real interest in the welfare of his charges and who manumitted or freed them when he could afford to do so. Most of the freedmen stayed right on as employees on the Nixon plantations, and there is no record of any slave ever having attempted to escape or to leave.

The exact date has been lost in the frequent retelling, but it seems that on one occasion the dreaded white plague, which was the name given in those days to the disease we know today as tuberculosis, visited the plantations in eastern North Carolina. It spread like wildfire from plantation to plantation and threatened to decimate the slave population of that area. The landowners were not immune to the ravages of the disease, and its coming spread fear before it. Little was known about the disease

65

in those days, and practically nothing about any treatment for it.

Mr. Nixon had the faith in the healthful qualities of the Outer Banks that his descendants have inherited from him in such large measure. He determined to use these qualities, no matter what the expense, to try to save the lives of his slaves. At considerable cost, he took carpenters and other laborers on board boat and floated lumber from Perquimans County down to Nag's Head, towing it with the currents, behind sailing barges. When they arrived, the carpenters proceeded to build a small village of weathertight houses, sheds, and outbuildings. These were generously spaced in the forest of hardwoods that stood on that spot in those days. Arbors were built on which to train the luxuriant local grapevines. Garden plots were cleared in the rich soil, and the earth was pulverized to make it ready for the seeds that were brought along.

Once this village was complete, Mr. Nixon returned to his plantations and chose from his slaves seven sisters whose families had been stricken with tuberculosis. He transported these seven sisters with their husbands and their children en masse to Nag's Head and set them up in housekeeping in the newly constructed village. Further, he stocked their pantries and smokehouses with food in abundance, as was his way. He brought several cows to their pastures and presented them with a whole herd of pigs.

There his slaves stayed in various stages of sickness and were administered to by doctors, who visited them regularly, and by boats from the plantations, which brought supplies. In the beginning, the healthier indi-

viduals had no duties other than fishing, clamming, crab-
bing, and tending their little garden plots, as well as
keeping house, while caring for the needs of the more
seriously sick of their number. As the ill ones began to
recover, however, the whole community took seriously
to fishing, gardening, and herding the cattle and swine.
Eventually the group became almost self-sufficient.

According to the story handed down from generation to generation, this Arcadian village lasted for a little
more than three years. It is said that not a single one of
the slaves died but that all the sick recovered, and there
were several births during that time. Upon their complete recovery, the whole community was brought back
to the plantations in Perquimans County, and the village
on the Outer Banks was abandoned, being soon retaken
by the forest.

The location of this ante-bellum health spa, this early
experiment in communal health care, is said to have been
on the exact spot where the seven lovely sand hills now
stand. It is from this settlement that the hills take their
name. Not long ago there were people who could tell
you what each hill was called, pointing out which hill
represented which sister. Unfortunately such detailed
knowledge has now been lost in the frenetic hurry and
bustle of our modern way of life.

Folk memory persists to the effect that those seven
sisters were the daughters of an African king and were
sold into slavery through the trickery and avarice of
certain court underlings who took advantage of an ill-
ness of the king to betray his family into the hands of
Yankee slave traders. Their mother died on board the
slave ship, so the legend goes, but the seven daughters

survived. They were sold in a lot on the auction block in Philadelphia and eventually found their way to the plantations of eastern North Carolina and to the owner-ship of this kind and humane master. The king lost no time in executing his betrayers, but by that time his wife and daughters were far beyond his reach and forever lost to him.

Admittedly it is untraditional and quite different from the usual conduct of ghosts, but the legend keeps com-ing back and back that the spirits of these seven prin-cesses return to this site of their great happiness and good fortune. This is said to occur always in the sum-mertime, the season of their greatest enjoyment of the Outer Banks.

To many it seems quite plausible that, on soft moonlit summer nights when the wind is still and the customary roar of the ocean is muted to a rhythmic sigh, you may see the ghost of one, or more, of these seven royal sisters walking the crest of her own namesake-hill and praying to whatever gods she knew for the recovery of her babies and her husband from the dreaded white plague. Such things can happen on these Outer Banks.

True, entomologists have long known that the ex-ceptionally brilliant fireflies denominated *Lampyridae Photinus* are found in great numbers on the flats behind these hills and are thought to migrate to the tops of the dunes on calm nights during certain periods in summer for their pyrotechnic courtship rites. Even the most dedicated and preoccupied practicing entomologist, however, would hardly confuse *Photinus* with the ghost of a princess.

8
HATTERAS JACK

For as many years as there have been deep water sailors, man has been fascinated by and strangely drawn to porpoises. Long before the advent of the internal-combustion marine engine and while navigators were still in bondage to the vagaries of wind and current, a rather large body of half-truth and half-legend grew up about these playful and intelligent kings of the deep.

Australia, for example, boasted of a very unusual specimen, who (not which, mind you, but who) met the early sailing ships carrying the prisoner-colonists to new homes on that continent and led the ships safely into sheltered anchorage. Pelorus Jack, as this purposeful porpoise was called, is as much a part of Australian legend as is the jolly swagman and his jimbuck.

At about the same time or possibly a little later in history (the exact times are not very clear) the Outer Banks of North Carolina had a similar phenomenon. Whereas the Australian porpoise was the standard brown and black, the Hatteras version was almost snow-white, a rare albino specimen. Whereas Pelorus Jack apparently contented himself with meeting and guiding inbound vessels, Hatteras Jack was a more versatile performer and greatly endeared himself not only to the pilots of Hatteras-bound vessels but to the permanent residents of those parts as well. With the exception of the short-lived porpoise fishery on Portsmouth Island, which was conceived and operated by outlanders for a few short months with only a few native boatmen as employees, the love affair between porpoises and the Outer Bankers has continued to this day.

North Carolina's Outer Banks are pierced at intervals by inlets where the waters of the Atlantic Ocean and the coastal sounds meet. Since the first attempts to settle this country, seafaring men have used these inlets to gain access to the mainland.

Many of the inlets known to ancient mariners have gradually closed up, so that they no longer exist except as names on very old maps. Examples of these are Raleigh's Inlet, which is said to have been located about nine miles north of the present Oregon Inlet, and, more recently, Caffey's Inlet, which used to exist a few miles north of the town of Duck.

Other openings in the banks appear to have become fairly permanent either by the action of man in stabilizing them or by the relatively fixed set of the currents that sweep through them. Such are Beaufort Inlet, which serves the Port of Morehead City, and Hatteras and Oregon inlets to the north.

Even with the best efforts of man and the relative predictability of the permanent currents, most inlets are treacherous and dangerous to shipping unless a local pilot cons the helm to avoid the ever-shifting shoals and reefs. This is true even in this day of sonar, warning

buoys, and flashing lights. It was true to an even greater degree in the days before these aids to navigation.

In the days of the pirate Blackbeard, Ocracoke Inlet was the customary gateway for ships wishing to come to safe anchor on the North Carolina coast. The town of Portsmouth was booming on the south shore of that inlet and was the trading center for the whole area. To the north lay Silver Lake, a safe and land-locked haven for the careening of ships. Later the majority of this traffic moved to Hatteras Inlet, some fifteen miles to the north, and this inlet remained the favorite for many years thereafter. It was here that the Confederate forts were built and here that the sea-borne Yankee invasion of the Civil War took place. Between the Revolution and the Civil War, Hatteras Inlet handled the vast majority of the ships and shipping trade for most of eastern Carolina.

This inlet, closest to the "Graveyard of the Atlantic," was then and remains today one of the most difficult to navigate. The topography of the sea and inlet bottom are constantly changing, and what may be a deep channel today can well be a dangerous reef next week. Most ships need deep water to stay afloat, at least deeper than the two or three feet over these ever-moving shoals and reefs. Deep water there is in Hatteras Inlet, but it is confined to a twisting, turning, and ever-changing channel. Snakelike it is in its complicated convolutions and continuous motion.

Imagine, if you can, the dilemma of those ante-bellum captains. With no auxiliary motor and only the power of the wind to propel them, they would creep with shortened sail into this inlet. With a sailor stationed in the chains, constantly heaving the lead line and calling out the decreasing depth, and with a lookout at the masthead, pointing out the breakers ahead, it is remarkable that any skipper would even attempt the passage.

It was about the year 1790 that help arrived upon the scene in the "person" of Hatteras Jack. Now, according to the tales that Hatterasmen tell when the winter winds are howling and they are sitting snug ashore around their warm stoves, Hatteras Jack was just as real as Edward Teach and a sight more helpful. While other porpoises contented themselves with sporting about the breakers and being mistaken for mermaids, Jack had a purpose in life.

That self-imposed duty, that high calling to which he was devoted, was the leading of ships into and out of Hatteras Inlet. He was the self-appointed pilot, and he never lost a ship during all of his long career. Captains of inbound ships would lie to off the inlet or else tack back and forth and wait for Hatteras Jack to put in an appearance. With the coming of high tide, there he would be, leaping clear of the water and swimming in figure-eights, his friendly grin just awash in the blue-green waters.

With a single prolonged blast on the ship's fog horn and an answering series of high-pitched squeaks from Jack, the piloting would begin. Slowly, now, so that the sailing boat would have no trouble in keeping up, Jack would head into the channel. Slowly he would swim through the various twists and turns of the channel-of-the-day, his white back gleaming just under the surface and the sailing vessel following in his wake. Carefully keeping to the very center of the deep water, Hatteras Jack would lead the vessel past the shoals, past the reefs, around the fishhook-shaped tip of Hatteras Island, and into the relatively safe waters of the Sound.

Once the escorted ship had come to rest and had let go her anchors with a roar of unwinding chain, the albino porpoise would go into a transport of glee, apparently at having concluded another successful mission. Unless there was another ship awaiting him outside the bar, he would then proceed to put on a show of tail-walking on the surface of the water, of complicated leaps and flips into the air, and of swift dartings and barrel-rolls just under the surface.

Hatteras Jack never sought, and apparently did not expect, any sort of reward from his human friends for services rendered. About the only reward he would have been interested in anyway, it was said, would have been a fish or two, but he was a much more accomplished fisherman than any human. The satisfaction of a job well done and the rendering of aid that only he could give are believed to have been the motivating reasons for his work. There are many things that man does not yet understand about porpoises. The instances of help that has been given man by this most intelligent of marine animals are legion and as yet not fully explained.

The story goes that our albino porpoise would carefully appraise each ship before undertaking the responsibility of guiding her into the inlet. If a ship appeared to be larger or more heavily laden than usual and thus deeper in the water, it is said that Hatteras Jack would literally take her measurements by diving on her port side, traversing the outline of her hull under water, and then surfacing on her starboard side. Thus, having sensed her draft and knowing well the depth of the water in the channel, he would know just how full the tide must be for that particular vessel to make a safe trip through the tricky channel.

No matter how many blasts were sounded on the fog horn, our guiding porpoise would steadfastly refuse to begin the trip until the tide had risen to a safe depth. While awaiting that hour, it is said, he would normally put on a show for the crew of the waiting ship. Sometimes alone and sometimes in company with other porpoises, he would exhibit the tremendous agility that porpoises possess and the keen sense of humor they are known to have. There were times, too, when he would engage in fights to the death with his mortal enemy, the shark. These combats were as spectacular as they were terrifying. Almost as much of the combat took place just above the surface of the water as occurred beneath it. The superior speed and intelligence of Hatteras Jack always brought him out the victor, and although the shark had terrible teeth and a savage will to fight, he was just no match for the porpoise.

This, then, is the story of Hatteras Jack—pilot, entertainer, warrior, and friend to man. This is the legend that has been handed down from generation to generation. This, plus the Outer Bankers' own happy experiences and encounters with present-day porpoises, is the reason why no real Outer Banker, native or adopted, will harm these creatures or permit them to be harmed if such harm can be prevented.

Call them bottle-nosed dolphin if you like; they are not fish, but mammals, which (or who) breathe air as we do, bear their young alive and nurse them at the breast, talk with each other in their own language, and have their own highly organized communities with laws which are rigidly obeyed. The brain of this remarkable animal is just as convoluted and complex as is the brain of man, and it is a great deal larger. One wonders what might have happened if the porpoise had had the advantage of an opposable thumb—but maybe he is much happier and better off as he is.

After buoys, lights, and bells or horns were put on platforms out in the inlet to mark the channel, Hatteras Jack just disappeared. He came back, they say, a time or two afterwards, as though he were checking all this newfangled equipment to see if it was really effective. He actually led a boat through the channel once in a while as though to keep his "fin in." His visits grew less frequent, however, and finally he stopped coming at all, but many still remember him and speak of him with love and with gratitude. He is part and parcel of their tradition. He, too, was a real Outer Banker.

9
LADY IN DISTRESS

Many and varied are the tales that are told of the lady Theodosia Burr Alston. Some are dull, and some exciting, but all of them end in tragedy. That she was an actual historical figure, there is not the slightest doubt. That she was a most pitiful and appealing person is also apparent. For years her fate was unknown and was the subject of much speculation, but, with the perspective of time, the pieces of the puzzle seem to fall into place. With the corroboration of several deathbed confessions by persons who should have known whereof they spoke, one can now deduce a fairly accurate picture of the beautiful, headstrong, and star-crossed lady.

Theodosia Burr was born to Aaron Burr and his wife in the city of Albany and raised in New York, then the capital of the young United States. While she was still a small child, her mother died, and Aaron determined to be both mother and father to her. He set out with the avowed intention of creating in his daughter his ideal of what the perfect woman should be. He himself was active in the highest circles of the national government of his country. His ambition and his political vision seemed to be unlimited, and his rise into political fortune seemed almost meteorlike in its dramatic brilliance.

Into the rearing of his child, this near-genius poured all the love and devotion he had felt for his wife, and out of his loneliness he drew the strength and dedication to do a superlative job. Burr envisioned his daughter as the perfect wife for some lucky man. She was to be so highly trained as to be a model of intelligence and charm, completely without the vacuity that characterized so many belles of the day. She was to be warm and understanding and able to be a real helpmeet to her husband at any and all levels of his life. Latin and Greek Burr taught her, as well as dancing and the harpsichord. She was as good at a game of chess as she was at working a pretty sampler.

Theodosia's eagerness in this training was matched only by her father's delight in her progress. She literally worshiped her talented father and wanted with all her young heart to be everything he wanted her to be. By the time she was twelve years old, this precocious child was already an accomplished hostess. By the age of sixteen, she was presiding at many of the most important receptions and other functions in the nation's capital.

Many suitors paid court to this remarkable girl. The scions of wealthy and influential families tried their best to win her hand in marriage; but to Theo, none of them could compare with her brilliant father. He outshone them all.

Then she met young Joseph Alston. Son of one of the finest families in South Carolina, he was reared in a tradition not unlike her own. He was intensely in-

terested in politics and government. His future seemed
bright and assured, and without doubt he loved Theodosia with all his heart. Youth called unto youth, and
the distinguished troth was plighted.

In one of the most dazzling social functions of this
country, Theodosia Burr became the bride of the Honorable Joseph Alston. After their wedding trip, the
couple removed to South Carolina, where, true to the
promise of his youth, Alston rose rapidly in the political
world and became Governor. One son was born, and
he was promptly named Aaron Burr Alston. According
to all reports, he was as lovely and charming a child as
one could well imagine.

Then the shadow of tragedy began to move across
the scene, and the family fortunes fell on darker days.
Aaron Burr, outstanding young statesman that he was,
became involved in a great political scandal. Alexander
Hamilton, another giant of the times, opposed Burr at
every turn and seemed to be his nemesis. Burr and
Thomas Jefferson were opposing candidates for the
Presidency of the United States, and the contest had
ended in a tie vote. Hamilton redoubled his efforts
against Burr, who, strangely, made no concerted effort
to overcome the tie with Jefferson. Jefferson and Burr,
therefore, each had seventy-three electoral votes, with
Hamilton doing all in his power to bring about Burr's
defeat and Burr remaining strangely silent. Ballot after
ballot was taken, and, finally, on the thirty-sixth ballot
the tie was broken. Thomas Jefferson became the third
President of the United States, taking office in the year
1801.

Burr remained silent no longer. Bitter in his disap-

79

pointment and goaded by the memory of Hamilton's opposition, he challenged Hamilton to a duel to the death. Hamilton did not want the duel and had it delayed several times, but Burr was adamant, and the two finally met on the "field of honor" on July 11, 1804, at the little town of Weehawken, New Jersey.

Now remember, Hamilton was the statesman who had insisted on the construction of lighthouses along the North Carolina coast. The lighthouse at Hatteras had been the direct result of his efforts and influence. To this day, many of the old-timers refer to it as "Hamilton's light."

As Hamilton and Burr descended from their carriages in the dim dawn and took their places on the greensward, the seconds asked each if the duel could not be averted and the matter settled without the drawing of blood. Burr shook his head, and Hamilton remained silent. As the signals were given, each of the antagonists raised and aimed his pistol. At the final signal, both fired almost simultaneously. Hamilton's shot went wide; but Burr fired with deadly accuracy, and Hamilton fell, mortally wounded. Thus was brought to an abrupt end the career of one of the most courageous and able statesmen of the young republic, and the Outer Banks lost one of its first and best friends.

A shocked and outraged citizenry demanded retribution for this act. Burr heard the political pack in full cry for his public life.

Rumors began to circulate that the onetime Revolutionary colonel was engaged in trying to stir up rebellion in the territories west of the Appalachian Mountains. Quickly the word spread that the former patriot was now bent upon the destruction of the country he had served.

History leaves us no room to doubt that Colonel Aaron Burr did, indeed, nourish ambitious and fantastic dreams of a secession of Kentucky and Tennessee from the United States, as well as a revolt of the Mississippi Territory and of the huge area later to be known as Alabama, Louisiana, and part of Texas, which had only recently been acquired by the young republic in the Louisiana Purchase.

Burr envisioned himself as the chief executive, possibly even the king, of this new nation, with the capital to be located in the city of New Orleans. Here he would preside (or reign) over a court of such brilliance as to put to shame the rather plain surroundings of President Thomas Jefferson in Washington. Even a military campaign to wrest Mexico and Florida from the Spanish was considered. Colonel Burr's vaulting ambition knew no bounds, and he was most indiscreet in talking about his dreams to people who he thought might be helpful.

Word of Burr's plans soon reached President Jefferson and the members of his Cabinet, and the time seemed ideal to lay a trap to catch the killer of Hamilton. Thus it was that when Burr took boat from Pittsburgh to travel down the Ohio and Mississippi rivers for New Orleans, one John Graham, an agent of Jefferson, trailed Burr in the hope of catching him in some overt act of treason.

The further south Burr progressed, the greater became the public support for his plans. This so alarmed Jefferson that he sent word ahead that the firebrand was to be arrested on sight for high treason.

Arrested in the Mississippi Territory, Burr willingly gave himself up to the civil authorities, claiming that he only intended the good of the western territories and the defeat and confusion of royalist Spain.

Tried in a Mississippi Territory court, Burr was acquitted of the charge of treason by a three-judge panel and released. Regardless of this, he was rearrested by federal troops several days later, put in irons, and transported the long, weary miles to Richmond, Virginia, where President Jefferson was determined he should stand trial again for high treason—this time in a federal court.

Once again the brilliant little Colonel was tried for high treason and for levying acts of war against the United States. Once again he was acquitted. One of the great landmarks of American law was erected here when John Marshall ruled in the pivotal decision of the case that "treason" and "levying war" against one's own country could be established only by an "overt act" in the first instance and by an "assemblage of men in preparation for battle" in the second. Thus was substantial justice achieved in that Burr was not convicted of treason, for the charges had been laid mainly because of the fatal duel with Hamilton. Dueling was the established order of the day, and to have perverted the law by punishing Burr for treason when what he had done was to kill a promising statesman would have been legal hypocrisy of the lowest kind. The orderly, precise mind of Marshall perceived this, and legal history was made.

Although his life was spared, Aaron Burr's political star had set. Broken in health and in spirit, he went into voluntary exile in England, where he stayed until the year 1812. Although he had been tried for treason, Burr loved his country, and when the clouds of war began to threaten and it became apparent that England would try to retake her former colony by force, Burr betook himself back to his beloved America and offered his services to her. Once again he attempted to regain a portion of his former influence and power as a leader in the political forums, but he met with rebuff after rebuff, and his failures made him heartsick.

In South Carolina, his daughter Theodosia had suffered for him during all his trials and misfortunes. As soon as she heard that he was coming back to this country, she made plans to visit him in New York. With all her heart she believed that she could cheer and encourage him at this time when he desperately needed someone to lean on. Her husband was still Governor of South Carolina and perhaps could be of some help. Plans for the visit were progressing but came to a complete halt when her only son, the handsome little Aaron Burr Alston, fell ill with the fever and died in her arms in June, 1812.

This loss left Theodosia prostrate in both mind and body. For a while her life as well as her sanity were despaired of. Youth and natural vigor prevailed, though, and she began to mend. Although still terribly depressed in spirit, she began to eat and to move about her former duties. By late fall of that same year she was beginning to talk once again of her desire to see her father in New York. She felt that she now needed him almost as much as he needed her.

In the hope that it might revive her spirits and make her once again the vivacious and charming young woman she had once been, her husband made arrangements for her to take the trip to New York to see her father. Although the War of 1812 was raging at the time and British warships were patrolling the entire coast, these were still the days of chivalry in warfare, and Governor Alston knew that any ship engaged on such a mission as his would be passed unharmed through the British blockade, particularly if it carried a letter from the Governor himself addressed to the honor of the British navy.

Thus, in December, 1812, the good ship *Patriot* was commissioned and sailed, unarmed, from the harbor of Georgetown en route to New York. Aboard were the lady Theodosia Burr Alston and her personal maid. In her luggage was a beautiful oil portrait of herself which she had had painted and which she intended to give to her father. As she left Georgetown, Theodosia seemed more animated and excited than she had in many months. Already the trip seemed to be doing her good. The portrait was hung on the wall of her private cabin, and the young traveler was made comfortable by her devoted maid.

The *Patriot* was not many days out of Georgetown when, sure enough, she was hailed and stopped by British men-of-war. An inspection party came aboard, and the British commander was presented with the letter of Governor Alston requesting safe passage for his wife through the blockade. As a courtesy to the lady and to the Governor of South Carolina, the *Patriot* was not even searched but was permitted to continue on her way and was wished Godspeed on her trip to New York.

Northward the *Patriot* sailed and into threatening

weather. She passed Cape Hatteras, plainly marked by Hamilton's light, under shortened canvas; and as she left the light on the larboard quarter, the storm increased. For two days she lay hove-to behind a drogue and waited for the storm to blow itself out. By the evening of the third day the wind had subsided, and the sea was somewhat calmer; but the sky was still heavily overcast, and the Captain had no idea just where he might be off the North Atlantic coast. With shortened sail and with lookouts at the masthead and in the chains, the *Patriot* cautiously probed her way through the darkness.

"Sail ho," came the cry from the masthead, "broad off the larboard beam." The helmsman and all others on deck immediately turned to the left and scanned the darkness. Just about broadside off the larboard side of the ship was a light that apparently could only mean another ship—a ship that could probably give them their exact position, no matter whether she was British or American. They had letters of safe conduct from the one and political identity with the other. Moreover, the light was barely moving; and its slow, easy rolling indicated to them that the lighted ship was in all probability lying at anchor.

Anxious for a chance to verify his position, the Captain of the *Patriot* recalled his watch from the chains, ordered his ship brought about, and headed in the direction of the light. Not wanting to take the risk of missing her, he ordered the *Patriot* to proceed under full sail and at best speed.

A bow wave formed under the forefoot of the trim little craft, and her wake gurgled from the speed of her passage. Not until they were within hailing distance of the presumed friendly light did the captain and crew realize to their horror that they were in the breakers. They had fallen prey to the old, old trick of the land pirates—the pirates of Nag's Head.

Hard aground rammed the *Patriot* on the outer bar in a welter of surf. Harder aground she lunged with each succeeding wave, more desperately and hopelessly lost. As the masts, under the pressure of the wind on full canvas, snapped off even with the deck, the mariners heard a new and more horrible sound. It was the screaming and cursing of the pirates as they put off through the surf in their small boats, not to rescue but to pillage and to kill. Up and over the sides of the helpless vessel they came, as motley and desperate a crew as can be imagined, but brave and cunning fighters every one. Up and down the decks of the *Patriot* they fought with the officers and men of the vessel until the scuppers of the doomed ship ran with blood. No sooner was a man cut down, whether pirate or sailor, than he was dumped overboard. In one awful half-hour every officer and seaman of the ship's company was ruthlessly murdered.

Theodosia, emerging from her cabin in fright when the *Patriot* had first run aground, watched in horrified disbelief. Her faithful maid was seized and thrown heartlessly overboard to the gathering sharks already tearing savagely in an orgy of blood lust at everything in the water. She went without a scream, without a word, without an outcry of any sort—her eyes fixed steadily upon those of her lovely young mistress. Then the pirates—dirks and swords red with blood—turned toward Theodosia, who stood cowering against the little superstructure of the cabin.

Already weakened by past sorrows and reeling from the sight of so many heartless acts of murder, the gentle mind of Theodosia Burr Alston took refuge in insanity. From that moment forward, and for as long as she lived, Theodosia was insane.

The land pirates, as have many primitive people before them since time began, respected that insanity. Moreover, they respected the person of Theodosia Burr Alston as one especially touched of God. Thus they feared to harm her, afraid of instant and violent retribution from above.

Gently, almost lovingly, they handed her down into a waiting surfboat and took her to shore. She took with her only one possession: the handsome oil portrait of herself which she had intended as a gift for her father.

The land pirates took the demented young woman into their homes. From home to home she went as the months passed, always welcome but free to go or stay as her childlike fancy led her. The simple Bankers cared for her as though she were a daughter and saw to it that she lacked nothing that they could provide. She never tried to leave the Island, never tried to run away. A vacant look held those lovely eyes, once sparkling with so much intelligence. To all greetings, all inquiries, her one reply was, "I am going to visit my father in New York." In her favorite fishing cottage where she stayed most often, the oil portrait hung at the place of honor over the mantel in the main room. It had replaced the shell of a huge horseshoe crab her hosts had formerly kept there. Often and for long minutes she would stand and stare at the picture as if trying to remember what it was and what significance it held for her. Always she would end such a scrutiny with a puzzled shake of her head and a weary sigh.

Thus the days passed, and the months, and the years. Some days were happy and some were periods of deep, black depression. Our castaway remained reasonably healthy, but there was no apparent improvement in her mental condition. After the last of the pirates had died or moved away, the fishermen took up the care of this pitiful woman and provided for her to the best of their ability. Theirs were acts of love and pity, rather than fear, and she was treated with unfailing kindness and generosity.

Many years later when Theodosia was an old, old woman and sick abed, Dr. William G. Poole, from Elizabeth City, whose kindly habit it was to visit the Outer Banks at intervals, came by the cottage where she was then staying. The doctor had treated her several times in the past without hope or expectation of fee. Often he had admired the oil portrait over the mantel and had wondered about its origin. Theodosia's hosts had offered him the portrait on several occasions, but he had always refused.

On this night, when once again the winds were wailing in their lonesome fury and the waves were beginning to pound in ever-increasing force up and onto the beach, the doctor had given Theodosia a mild sedative, and she was apparently asleep, completely relaxed and snoring gently. As he turned to go, the head of the household took the portrait down from the wall and held it out to him. "Take it, doctor," the fisherman said. "It is little enough to give you for all the times you have helped her. If she were in her right mind, I know she would insist on your having it. Maybe you can sell it in Elizabeth City or in Norfolk. Take it as your fee."

Even as the good doctor shook his head in refusal, Theodosia leaped from her bed and, with a piercing shriek, snatched the picture from the hands of the fisherman. "It is mine. It is mine," she screamed. "You know I am going to visit my father in New York, and this is to be his picture—his picture of his Theo."

Grasping the portrait to her breast, she then ran out of the room so quickly that they could not detain her—out into the storm and down toward the pounding surf. In vain they followed—the doctor, the fisherman and his wife and children—to try to prevent her injury. Theodosia disappeared into the driving mist and spume of a howling, raging wind. They never saw her again.

Theodosia's body was never found. The ocean had claimed her for its own. The deep prints of her running feet led down to the sea's edge but did not return. Next day, however, at high tide, the portrait was found just a short distance down the shore from where Theodosia had last been seen. All agreed that it should be given to the doctor. He reluctantly took it and promised to see if he could have it identified. The lady in the picture was obviously a person of wealth and breeding. The gown in which she was portrayed had an expensive look, and the few jewels were in excellent taste.

No sooner had the doctor gotten it back to the city than numerous people began to recognize it as being an excellent likeness of the lost Theodosia. Contact was made with the Burr family, who were told about the picture. Several members of the family made a special trip south to see it. They, too, identified the girl in the portrait as none other than the wife of the Governor of South Carolina, the ill-fated Theodosia Burr Alston.

The finding of the portrait made all the newspapers of the day. Then three old men of the sea were reported, on separate occasions and in different cities, to have made deathbed confessions that they had taken part in the looting of a ship lured onto the Outer Banks between Christmas and New Year's in the year 1812. Each of them confessed in penitence that all the ship's company had been killed, that one young woman had been thrown to the sharks, and that the mind of another had been taken by God.

The portrait was treasured by Dr. Poole as long as he lived and was kept in his home. At his death it was inherited by his granddaughter, Mrs. John P. Overman, also of Elizabeth City.

Today the battered but still beautiful portrait has been preserved for those to whom it rightfully belongs, the American people. It hangs now in a place of honor in the Macbeth Art Gallery in New York City, where it is proudly identified as the young Mrs. Alston. Thus has Theodosia's portrait finally completed its journey to the town for which it was destined.

Is it more than just a coincidence that the slayer of the creator of Cape Hatteras Light should, in turn, lose his most precious possession, his only child, to the false lights displayed on those same Outer Banks? Whether this wild and beautiful region struck back in revenge for the senseless killing of one of its first and greatest friends is, of course, beyond pondering. Many people will assure you that if you walk the Nag's Head beach during the dreary season between Christmas and New Year's;

if you choose a time when the sky is overcast and the wind whines up from the wildness of the North Atlantic and blows wraiths of spume and spindrift along the beaches, you may see Theodosia. She will not harm you. She was always a gentle person. There she walks, they say, looking—ever looking—for that handsome portrait she longs to carry to her father in New York.

10
THE DEVIL'S HOOFPRINTS

*About twelve miles east of the "original" town of Wash-*ington in eastern North Carolina is the pleasant little town of Bath. Partially restored now through the efforts of public-spirited and history-conscious people of the section, it is a charming replica of the town as it originally looked. This is the way it appeared when Governor Eden maintained the capital of North Carolina there and when Edward Teach, the notorious pirate Blackbeard, roamed the sounds and estuaries of the Tar Heel State before the American Revolution.

Some there are who say that the ghost of Blackbeard still roams these waters and tramps the midnight streets of this restored colonial town in search of his head, which Lieutenant Maynard long since carried back to Virginia. It seems probable that pirate and governor were business partners, and there are people who still maintain that Eden owed his associate better protection than he got, or at least a warning that Maynard was coming. They even go so far as to suggest with a knowing wink not only that Governor Eden knew of Maynard's expedition but also that a large amount of Blackbeard's undivided treasure reposed in Eden's cellar at the time, and this helps to explain the extraordinary failure of gubernatorial protection. Since it is not recorded that any heirs of the headless pirate came forward to claim a portion of this supposed cache, it seems only logical to assume that, if there were, indeed, any undivided profits at the time, they must have remained in the private treasury of the governor.

Some years later, in fact after the Revolution but before the War Between the States, and in this same history-haunted neighborhood of Bath, there sprang up a legend that is almost unique, since the folk memory of the area is clear and in substantial agreement about it. Further, the physical phenomena involved are still right there in the open for anyone to see. "In the open" is perhaps an inappropriate figure of speech because the apparently deathless death marks are in a wooded area, but they are plain enough to see and easy enough to get to. One can literally do his own research and draw his own conclusions.

In the year 1850, so the story goes, there lived near Bath Town a gentleman by the name of Elliott, who owned a stallion of which he was very proud, and quite justly so. Tradition has it that this was the fastest race horse in that part of the State and that it had shown its heels to every other animal it had raced against.

It seems that one Sunday afternoon Elliott, while in his cups, was preparing this noble stallion for a race to be held the following day on the town commons in Bath. A part of the preparation was to have been a trial run around the race track on the commons. Although already unsteady on his feet, Elliott had saddled and

mounted his fine steed and was on his way the short distance to Bath when he observed in the road ahead a horse
almost as magnificently muscled as his own. That there
was such a horse in these parts came as a complete surprise. What was more, the rider of the horse rode with
such skill and grace that he seemed almost a part of the
animal. Horse and rider made such a pretty picture of
equestrian excellence that Elliott urged his own mount
forward to overtake them.

He discovered that both were travelers from afar, although the face of the rider seemed strangely familiar,
yet peculiar and almost unreal. The penetrating gaze
from the stranger's hard, cruel eyes might have sent a
shiver of apprehension through a less inebriated person.
After introductions, the two horsemen rode on side by
side along the narrow, tree-shaded lane. The unusual
horseman informed Elliott that he, too, was on his way
to Bath to find lodging for his horse and himself. Further, the stranger averred that he planned to enter the
race on the morrow and had every expectation of win-
ning. One word led to another about the relative merits
of the two horses until the quick-tempered Elliott sug-
gested in no uncertain terms that there was no necessity
to wait for the morrow. The road on which they were
traveling was straight and level, and the issue should be
settled immediately as to which horse was the faster.
The stranger readily agreed.

So far as is known there was no formal wager made,
but worshipers walking home from a protracted meeting at a nearby church distinctly heard Elliott say in a
loud voice that he intended to win the race or else to
drive his horse to hell in the attempt. These church peo-

ple had just left the hours-long session in which they had heard several visiting preachers in turn exhort their listeners to repentance and confession. They had seen several friends and neighbors go forward to kneel at the altar in witness to their conversion. Since the thoughts and conversation of these strollers as they moved homeward along the tree-shaded road were of the religious matters they had heard and seen that day, the rough language of the horseman fell with added impact on their ears. The stranger's answer was spoken in a low voice and was not understood, but there was no forgetting the sinister smile that played about his mouth nor the unearthly, calculating gleam in his eyes.

Both riders laid the whip to their horses, and the two splendid beasts sprang into full gallop, side by side, scattering the alarmed pedestrians into the road ditches. On the horses raced, full-out now and matching stride for stride, their taut bellies almost touching the road beneath, their nostrils flared wide in search for breath, and their riders standing in the stirrups with shoulders and heads crouching over flying manes.

Nobody knows exactly what happened then. Some say they heard a curse from Elliott, and others vow the evil-looking stranger uttered an awful, demoniac laugh. One thing is clear. Whatever the reason, Elliott's beautiful stallion suddenly whinnied as though in terror, then shied to its right, ran completely off the road, and leaped prodigiously into the air, throwing Elliott with great force against a large pine tree and killing him instantly. The horse died almost at the same instant of a broken neck.

In the great excitement that prevailed at the death

scene, the stranger was forgotten for a few minutes. When he was remembered, he was nowhere to be found, nor was he ever seen in Bath Town. Some of the witnesses to the tragedy followed the tracks of the other rider's horse to a point in the road that was opposite the place where Elliott lay. There the stranger's tracks ended abruptly in mid-road. They did not continue either in the road or in the soft soil alongside.

Although this was a Sunday when there would be no distilling of turpentine anywhere in the county, there was an immediate, strong, and fresh smell of burning pitch, which lingered for some time around the death scene.

As though this were not mystery enough, the four hoofprints where Elliott's stallion had sprung into his leap of death remained gouged into the ground near the large pine forty or more feet off the road. They were still there the next morning, and the next week, and the following year. They are there right now as you read these lines. It seems impossible to erase them.

In 1925 the writer spent the night camped out where these seemingly permanent horse tracks are located. He thoroughly covered the tracks with dirt and began his nightlong vigil, propped against a large pine. The object, of course, was to watch those tracks all night long to see if they would uncover themselves. Now, certain it is that he nodded briefly during the night, but only briefly. By the early light of dawn he made an eager examination of the terrain. There the tracks were, sharp and clear and deep again, just as though they had never been covered.

Well does he remember the sensation of hackles rising

on the back of his neck as primordial fear struggled to assert itself. Equally well does he recall the sense of blessed relief in suddenly beholding an early fisherman trudging along the road on the way to Bath Creek. He has made many return visits over the years since that day and has always found the tracks intact. His last visit, made some thirty days before this writing, found them just as deep and clear as they were more than thirty years ago.

Mrs. Myrtle Cutler Jones of Blount's Creek, North Carolina, whose father once owned this land, remembers when her grandfather, a God-fearing and truthful man, built a hog pen around and enclosing these tracks. She remembers that the hogs would never eat corn that fell in the tracks, nor would they disturb the hoof-shaped depressions.

Debris placed in the prints will be found outside them the next morning. Birds will not eat corn or other grain placed in the imprints, although they will gobble up such delicacies spread around outside the curved tracks. Most of the residents in that area know about the tracks and accept them at face value as did their grandparents and great-grandparents.

At one time these hoofprints of Elliott's stallion became so famous that some gentleman put up a little stand, built a fence around the tracks, and charged admission to go in and see them. The concrete slab that was the foundation of the ticket booth is still there. The booth itself has long since deteriorated and been moved away. As of this writing the tracks are open for public inspection without charge whatsoever. There they remain, staring back at the observer.

Seemingly permanent, they are located just a few yards from the Camp Leech Road in the immediate vicinity of Bath, North Carolina, and you can drive your automobile to within fifty feet of them without even getting off the pavement.

11
SWANQUARTER INCIDENT

If you stand on the shore of Ocracoke Inlet and look
directly north-northwest across the waters of Pamlico
Sound, you will, if your vision is good enough, be looking across some thirty miles of open water at the lovely
little coastal town of Swanquarter, North Carolina.

How long Swanquarter has been a fishing village no
one knows. Some of the earliest records of colonial
America mention this little settlement of fishermen who
wrested their living from the often turbulent waters of
Pamlico Sound. Although geographically on the mainland, it is in spirit and in history part and parcel of the
Outer Banks of North Carolina. Long before there were
any roads at all in eastern North Carolina, there was
frequent commerce between this town and the fisher
folk who inhabited the seashore yonder in the distance.
Many a young swain has sailed the thirty or more moonlit miles to go a-courting his lady love. If you think
giving out of gasoline while wooing one's beloved in
an automobile is romantic, how would you react to
being becalmed and motionless in a boat with your in-

tended upon a mirror-like expanse of smooth water silver-plated by a full moon?

In the 1870's, the fishermen, merchants, and other residents of Swanquarter decided that the time had come when they should have a central place of worship and that, to supplement the cottage prayer meetings which had been going on for generations, they should build a house of God. What they wanted was a church, a building to be used only for the worship of God, for their spiritual enrichment, and for the proper upbringing of their children.

Enthusiasm for the project mounted, and plans were made for the size and type of structure they wanted. Those of the village who were experienced in masonry and carpentry had agreed to give of their time and skill. Others pledged to contribute in various ways, mostly in kind, because what money they had was to be spent for the purchase of a plot of land, which was to become holy ground—the ground upon which they would build their church.

The location committee worked long and diligently, examining various possible sites for the building. They finally agreed unanimously that the one site they most preferred was a corner lot that overlooked the town and had a distant view of beautiful Swanquarter Bay. There was only one such lot vacant, but it was amply large for their purposes.

After reporting to the entire congregation and receiving their approval, the committee called upon the owner of the lot and told him of their plans and of their desire to purchase the site. To their disappointment, however, the owner gave them a polite but firm refusal.

The land was not for sale, he said. He had other plans and purposes for the site and was just not interested in selling, and, even if he were induced to alter his long-range plans, he could not and would not permit the church people to pay such an unreasonably high price as he would have to charge for the lot. He was sincere about it. He plainly and honestly told the committee that he was certainly not using this as a device to hike the price of the lot but was just not interested in selling. To prove his sincerity, he even offered to help them find another lot that they would like as well.

Sadly disappointed but courteous in their frustration, the committee departed to report their failure to the congregation, and the search was resumed, this time for a "second-best" location. In time, such a place was found, the purchase made, and construction of the long-awaited church begun. One of the prime movers in the project was a man named B. G. Credle, who had been reared in Swanquarter and had lived there all his life. Later he removed to the city of New Bern to live.

The "second-best" lot was purchased at a moderate price from a man named J. W. Hayes. The foundations of the church were laid, and the floor and framework erected thereon. Work moved slowly because the builders had first to provide for their own families and could work on the church building only as their time would permit. So anxious, however, were the people to begin using the building that they started holding worship services there just as soon as it was closed in from the weather. Happy were they that God's people finally had even a partially completed house of worship where they could gather on the Lord's Day. They praised God for His wonderful works and His innumerable mercies and blessings to all men, but particularly to those who go down to the sea in ships.

By September, 1876, the congregation was worshiping in a nearly completed building. The older people will tell you that, at this time, Almighty God Himself decided to take a hand in the affairs of the church.

It is a matter of official record and is amply documented in both the business and the personal diaries of that day that, on September 16, 1876, a terrific storm began brewing on the Outer Banks of North Carolina. Rain fell in torrents, and the wind steadily increased until it was blowing first a full gale and then a hurricane. The little village of Swanquarter battened down and prepared to ride it out as it had in past storms. This time, however, the gale seemed to hold, blowing directly inland from the mouth of Swanquarter Bay and causing the backed-up waters of that estuary to flood the streets of the town in ever-deepening tides.

On the morning of September 17, the wind had reached such a velocity and the flooding tide such a depth in the town that the new church building was actually blown from its foundations and floated free, like a boat, at the mercy of wind and tide.

Remarkably, and to the great astonishment of many people, this water-borne building seemed to be sailing a definite course. It did not cut across vacant lots and corners but sailed determinedly down the street, gathering speed all the while and wavering neither to the right nor to the left. As those seafaring witnesses would have put it, "She was sailing full and by, directly before the wind."

On it sailed until it bore down upon and collided with Mr. Credle's general store, which was still fast on its foundations. This store was owned by a relative of the B. G. Credle who had been so active in the construction of the church. As soon as the sailing building struck the store, it turned at right angles to its former course and crossed a deep, swift-flowing canal. It came then to a halt, stopped apparently by some small saplings which did not seem nearly strong enough to halt the progress of such a large object as a church building.

The saplings were on the very lot that the building committee had unsuccessfully tried to buy, the location where all had agreed they would most like to have their church. As the waters began to recede and the wind to slacken, the church settled and came to rest in the center of the lot, facing the street: exactly where the congregation had wanted to build it in the first place. Truly, God moves in mysterious ways his wonders to perform. "After all," the members still say to this day, "does not God own the wind and the water? Is it so remarkable that He should use His tools to work His will?"

The lot owner himself had recognized God's hand in this deed. Without even waiting for the waters to completely subside, he got out his boat, rowed to the house of the chairman of the building committee, and assured him that if the church would send a delegation to meet him at the Courthouse, he would be glad to donate the lot free of charge and would even loan his building-jacks so that the structure could be raised and a foundation placed under it.

When the water dropped to the point where they could get into the Courthouse, the gift deed was passed, underpinning was installed, and new front and rear steps were built to the church. The worship of God was then taken up on the new site. Local residents recall that when the first services were held in the new location, the attending crowd was so large that chairs had to be brought and placed in the churchyard outside the building to accommodate the overflow of people.

When this church was dedicated, it was decided to call it Providence Church. So it was named, and so it is known now. When the church membership grew so large that a new building had to be constructed, the old building was sold to a neighbor to be used as a barn. After the death of the late Mr. and Mrs. W. T. Berry, however, their children presented this historic old building back to Providence Church and had it moved again (by land this time) to the church lot.

Today this building stands on the church lot and is used as a Sunday School Department. Its present location, if you are interested in going to see it, is just to the rear of the new brick building that now houses Providence Church. Renovated under the supervision of the Reverend R. Z. Newton, former pastor, it is known today as the Berry Memorial Building.

Try to tell some of the residents of Swanquarter that this church was not moved by the hand of God. Try to convince them that it was coincidence or happenstance that guided the sailing church along its complex route until it came to rest upon the exact lot on which they had wanted to build it in the first place. You try, if you like.

They are gentle people, and about the worst response that you could cause in them would be a slow, pitying smile, as they sadly shake their heads and walk away from you.

12
THE WITCH OF NAG'S HEAD WOODS

Early in the nineteen hundreds there lived in a bosky
dell in Nag's Head Woods a genuine witch. No fig-
ment of the imagination was this, but a real, flesh-and-
blood woman who lived alone in a very witchlike
cabin, covered, top and sides, with dark cedar shingles.
She shared this cabin with a coterie of black cats.

If beauty lies in the eye of the beholder, then the
ability to practice witchcraft certainly lies in the credu-
lity of the believer. Of these last there were a goodly
number. After all, witchcraft was not one whit more
remarkable than what those Wright fellows had done
over yonder at Kill Devil Hill a year or so ago.

The name of the lady was Miss Mabe (pronounced to
rhyme with Abe), and her cabin was very near the
shore of Roanoke Sound. She had the most spine-chilling
cackle you can imagine and a sharp, piercing eye. She
was very kind to children and would tell your fortune
for a coin—any kind of coin. She always foretold good
things for children—candy and fishing trips and the like
—and a surprising number of them came to pass.

It was an ante-bellum (First World Bellum, that is)

parlay par excellence, therefore, for a child to crawl under the elevated porches of Hollowell's Store at the foot of the Sound-side steamboat wharf to search for such coins. The coins occasionally fell from the pockets of porch strollers and disappeared through the wide cracks between the boards into the sand beneath, where they became fair game for all children. A child who found a coin would clutch it tightly in a sweaty palm and then secrete it until some indulgent adult would agree to take him into Nag's Head Woods to see the black cats, to pay his coin, and to stand wide-eyed and deliciously frightened as his very own fortune was foretold.

Children were not the only ones who knew Miss Mabe was a witch. Many of the fishermen who lived on the shore line of Roanoke Sound knew it, too, though they sometimes forgot it to their sorrow.

From the porch of her house a flimsy pier stretched out into the deeper water of the boat channel. It was the gracious custom of each fisherman of the area to slow his boat as he passed near her pier and throw thereon several of the choicest fish from his day's catch. She appreciated this and would always call out her thanks and a special blessing on both him and his boat as he sped off up the Sound toward his home.

There were days, though, when things did not go so well offshore; when the fishermen were so preoccupied that they would forget to share with her. On these rare occasions Miss Mabe's anger was awesome to behold. She could and often did retaliate for such neglect by changing the direction of the wind so that they could not get outside to fish in the ocean.

To do this, she would soak a cloth mop in kerosene, set it afire, and then, holding the mop handle like a torch with the end blazing brightly, run three times around her little cabin, intoning in a piercing, cracked voice:

> When the wind is from the south,
> It blows the bait in the fish's mouth.
> An' when the wind is from the west,
> That's when fishing is the best.
> When the wind is from the east,
> That's when fishing is the least.
> But when the wind is from the north,
> Then the fisherman can't go forth.
> Ah—ha—ha—ha—haaaaaaaaaaa—Hah!

As she completed the third circuit of her cabin, she would run rapidly to the corner that pointed in the direction from which she wanted the wind to blow—usually the northeast. There, some five or six feet from the cottage wall, she would drive the handle of the still-burning mop down into the sand while emitting that last "Hah!" and there the blazing torch would stand alone until it burned out.

There are many fishermen, still alive and vigorous, who will tell you that the wind invariably changed within twelve hours after she did this and that it always came about to blow from the direction she had commanded. Of course, so long as she made the wind blow strongly from the northeast, very little fishing could be done. It was the usual thing for a delegation of fishermen to call upon her after about three consecutive days of such weather to see if they could remedy the wrong. After promising not to forget her the next time they had large catches of fish and after imploring her to change the wind back to a more favorable quarter, they would take their leave, return home, put their nets in order—and their lines—and wait confidently.

Now, Miss Mabe never promised them to change the wind back, and she never expected or accepted any payment when the wind did change. She would tell the fishermen that she was just a poor widow woman, but she would see what, if anything, she could do. That's all she would ever promise them. Without fail, however, the wind always did come back around to the south or west, and the fisher-fellows could go out again with their nets and lines. One of the more remarkable things about such a change in the weather was that the fishing always seemed to be much better after than it had been before the onset of the foul weather which had kept them ashore.

Many people would then say they believed more strongly than ever that Miss Mabe was a good woman at heart; that she really didn't like to bring the wind out of the northeast. They would aver, moreover, that honest fishermen ought to be ashamed of themselves when they had a splendid catch of fish but then forgot to share it with a woman who had no way to catch fish of her own.

13
A DOOR FOR ST. ANDREWS

As every history student knows, Christianity was first brought to the area that is now known as eastern North Carolina and Virginia by British seafarers. History tells us that, other than the Roman Catholicism of the Spanish settlers in the colonial territory then known as New Spain, this was the first sustained introduction of the Christian religion into the New World of the Americas. Thus it fell to the lot of the Church of England—at that time the state church under the reign of Queen Elizabeth and later Americanized as the Episcopal Church of the United States—that it should be the first bearer of the Protestant version of the "good news" of the gospel of Jesus Christ to American shores. (The State of California claims to the contrary that Sir Francis Drake and his crew of the *Golden Hind* held church services on a Pacific beach before the date of the landing of the Sir Walter Raleigh colonists, but Drake's worship was not sustained or established in the form of a permanent chapel or church building.)

Thus it was that the baby, Virginia Dare, first English child to be born in America, was duly christened in the

"Citie of Ralegh" on Roanoke Island in 1587. Indian Chief Manteo had been baptized only a few days earlier at the same partially completed church.

After this auspicious beginning, the Episcopal Church in America suffered a series of setbacks. When Governor John White returned to Roanoke in 1590 in his vain search for Eleanor and Virginia Dare, he found that the chapel had been partially razed and then abandoned to the ravages of nature and the encroaching forests. Many years were to pass before another Episcopal chapel was erected near Roanoke Island, more than twenty years were to pass before regular Church of England services were being held in the little settlement of Jamestown in what is now Virginia, and some thirty years were to elapse before the Pilgrims' debarkation at Plymouth Rock. These, then, were the very beginnings, the wellsprings, of Protestantism in America.

There are records of itinerant preachers of various other Protestant denominations holding religious services in the homes of fishermen in the general area of Roanoke as early as the year 1670. It is certain that small Protestant churches were built on the North Carolina mainland thereabouts as early as 1698. The present Methodist Church in the village of Kitty Hawk has ancient beginnings, as do other Protestant churches on the shores of Albemarle Sound, but it was not until the late seventeen hundreds that another Episcopal church was erected by worshipers in the Walter Raleigh Coastland. The new edifice was doomed to suffer a fate similar to the one of the original chapel.

During the War Between the States (in 1865, to be exact) the church was once again torn down and destroyed. This time, it was not Indians who did the leveling, but Union troops, under the command of General Ambrose Burnside. Under the orders of that hirsute commander, the church was systematically ripped apart, board by board, and such timber as remained usable was incorporated into the construction of crude huts to shelter the many runaway slaves who were thronging to Roanoke Island at the time. The timbers that were badly damaged and broken were cut up and used for firewood for the Federal troops occupying Roanoke Island. Their commander was the same General Burnside who started the fashion for men of the day of letting their whiskers grow down their cheeks to form sideburns, or "Burnsides" as they were then known.

Having been once again deprived of their church, the Episcopalians, with the help of other denominations, continued to hold their services, sometimes in private homes, sometimes in churches borrowed for a day, or occasionally on the open beach with the Atlantic Ocean for a backdrop.

Years after the Civil War ended, Congress was asked to make some sort of reparation for the destruction of this church. The claim was ignored for many years, but early in the twentieth century, the lawmakers got around to granting the request. They awarded the princely sum of exactly $700.00 for the construction of a new church.

One of the dedicated, saintly men who held the members together during the years from the eighteen-nineties through 1916 was the "Viking Vicar," the Reverend Dr. Robert D. Drane, of Edenton parish. He regularly sailed his boat, the *Skipjack*, from Edenton to the Dare coast and there conducted church services in his own cottage, in the homes of others, in ballrooms, and sometimes on the ocean beach itself. He was one of those chiefly responsible for the reparation grant from Congress, which finally came through in 1915.

With the pitifully small sum of $700.00, augmented by such contributions as the summer cottagers could make, and with labor furnished largely by willing communicants among the native population, work went forward during 1915 and 1916 to erect the church that was to become St. Andrews by the Sea and that is now located on the ocean boulevard at about milepost 13. Originally located several hundred yards west of where it now stands, St. Andrews was built on the Sound side of Engagement Hill, the large sand dune that now looms softly behind the church. This was the logical location at the time, because most of the summer cottages were clustered around the wharf that ran out into Roanoke Sound and most of the year-round population lived either around the wharf or nearby in Nag's Head Woods.

Work progressed nicely on the church when the weather permitted. The workmen labored with love as well as with skill. Gradually a fine chapel took shape upon these historic sands.

By early 1916 the church was closed in, the roof was on, and the pews were in place. The altar and prayer rail were indeed works of beauty, hand-wrought with exquisite detail. So closely had the builders calculated and so well had they built that there was not a usable scrap of lumber left. The material had all been exhausted, and the money all spent, and St. Andrews by the Sea was complete—with one exception. There was no door. To make things worse, there was no money with which to buy a door, and the doorway itself was so generous in size and of such a shape that no second-hand door would do. No one seemed to know exactly how it happened, but the man who framed that doorway was indeed an artist. Quite possibly he was Arabian or at least of Moslem descent, since the generous size and beautiful proportions of the doorway, with its steeply arched, onion-shaped top, looked almost Indian-Moslem, reminiscent of the Taj Mahal or of the top of a minaret. Where on earth could a door be found to fit this large and unusual aperture? And if, perchance, such a door could be found, where was the money to come from to pay for such an expensive work of art?

Confronted with this emergency, Dr. Drane called a meeting and urged all interested parties to assemble at his cottage, rather than in the still-unconsecrated church. The meeting was so well attended that there was not room inside Dr. Drane's cottage for the crowd, and the proceedings were moved outside. The rector and a number of other people took their places on the porch, and the remainder of the rather large crowd stood or sat upon the sand between the cottage and the ocean. The purpose of the meeting was soon made known. The lack of a church door presented a pressing problem, and this prayer meeting had been called to ask the Almighty Himself for guidance.

Dr. Drane was not only a highly intelligent and well-educated man but also dedicated and very earnest, and he believed with all his heart and soul in the efficacy of sincere prayer. As this fine servant of God knelt upon the porch of his cottage, with his friends and co-workers kneeling around him and on the beach before him, he sought divine help for his fledgling church.

With deep reverence in every line of his kneeling figure and in every tone of his rich voice, this great and good man outlined the struggles of his people to build a place of worship and explained this last difficulty in the matter of a suitable door.

The meeting was soon concluded, and the throng began to disperse under a brilliant afternoon sunshine. The day was a beautiful one, with only a few fleecy clouds in the sky and just a gentle ground swell on the incredibly blue-green sea. It would have been a perfect day for a picnic, for a fishing trip, or for almost any other kind of outdoor activity. The sea was so tranquil under a soft, warm breeze it seemed unbelievable that it ever had been, or really could be, lashed by storm winds.

By nightfall that same evening the breeze had ceased, and a flat calm ensued. By midnight, however, the wind had hauled around to blow from the northeast, and by daybreak it was blowing a howling, whining full gale. The ocean was now churned into a writhing cauldron of huge waves pounding with the sound of thunder upon the beach. The air was full of spindrift and stinging, wind-driven rain, fog, and mist. The hungry sea piled higher and higher on the beach in a gigantic storm tide, as if it would once and for all swallow up this narrow sand reef and all that man had built upon it.

For three full days and nights the northeast gale raged and blew. People battened down, stayed snug and dry

inside their houses, and didn't even stick their noses outside if they could avoid it. By dawn of the fourth day
she had blown herself out, however; and the wind had
once again shifted to the southwest. A rather tall sea
was still running, but the sky was again practically
cloudless and a sparkling, brilliant blue and white. Thus
has it ever been at Nag's Head. The most gorgeous
weather that can be imagined always follows on the
heels of the wildest northeasters.

Now, remember, this was in 1915 and 1916. The
patriot Princip had killed the Archduke, and most of
the world was already plunged into the holocaust of
World War I. Since the United States had not yet been
drawn into the fighting, the war, to most of the country,
seemed remote indeed beyond the broad insulation of
the Atlantic Ocean, but the Outer Bankers knew a war
was going on. Almost daily they came into contact on
the beaches with grisly evidence of the savage U-boat
campaign being waged just offshore. There were many
nights when the eastern sky glowed red from the light
of burning ships, and strange and curious objects washed
ashore from the flotsam and jetsam of the battles.

One of the favorite hunting grounds of the U-boats
was the ocean just off Nag's Head, where the Labrador
Current and the Gulf Stream flowed in opposite direc-
tions but in close juxtaposition, offering to surface ships
the helping push of the appropriate current. Since the
shipping lanes lay close together, and the harried mer-
chantmen stayed as close to shore as they dared in their
efforts to avoid the deadly torpedoes, the hunting here
was often excellent. It was not unusual, in those days,
for wreckage to come ashore, even in calm weather; but

after a northeast storm, there would be even more. With this storm, Nature seemed to have outdone herself in a mighty effort to fling from the bosom of the sea all the wreckage, trash, and pollution that man had put there. The beach was littered for miles and miles with the most outlandish assortment of flotsam and jetsam ever seen at Nag's Head. There was not only wreckage from recent sinkings but also an assortment of parts from old wrecks which had obviously been under water for years. There was cordage, lumber, and fragments from cargoes of many and various kinds and descriptions.

Nag's Head, that day, was a beachcomber's paradise, but the most remarkable object of all had been carried by the storm tide almost to the very front step of Dr. Drane's cottage. There, at the high-tide mark, soaking wet and covered by a thin film of sand and one or two wisps of seaweed, was a door. Not an ordinary door, but a beautifully proportioned, large door, with a top so steeply and gracefully arched that its shape immediately reminded one of the beauty of the Taj Mahal. The beauty of the wood from which it had been constructed brought outbursts of admiration from many. Wonder of wonders, this door fitted exactly into the empty portal of the church, as if it had been made for that opening—and who is to say it was not! It was obviously a new, or at least an unused, door because there was no mark upon it to indicate that hinges had ever been fastened to its edges.

Why such a door was part of a deck cargo of a vessel in wartime, no one knew. How it happened to be lost at that particular time and in that very place will remain locked with the other secrets of Mother Sea. Such abstract considerations did not bother the church builders. They knew they had done their best, had built well, and, in spite of all their efforts, had come up one door short. An all-wise and almighty Father had seen their predicament, had taken pity upon them, and had supplied their exact need. It was as simple and as magnificent as that. It was not the first time that many of them had seen the hand of God move upon the face of the waters, and they did not expect it to be the last.

When the door had dried out, it was fitted to St. Andrews and, for years—as long as the church continued on the west side of Engagement Hill—was in daily use as the front door.

In later years population shifts took place at Nag's Head, and the people began to concentrate on the ocean side. To keep pace with the times and also to avoid being buried by the drifting Engagement Hill, the church was moved to its present location on the opposite, or eastern, side of the hill, close to the paved highway. It now lies between the two paved highways.

Since, in that day, the church had no narthex, a vestibule entrance was built on the front of the church, and a balcony on the inside. The massive door that had washed up was replaced by lighter and smaller swinging doors, which are in use on the church today.

If you should wish to attend services at St. Andrews by the Sea, or if you should just happen to go into the church for a few moments of quiet meditation (as you are most welcome to do at any time), look up over the top of the swinging doors as you leave. There, under the balcony, is the imprint of the top of the arched door, plainly discernible where the wall has been boarded up to make the smaller doors fit nicely. The difference in color and construction, far from being unattractive, stands as a sort of memorial to the simple, deep faith of those earlier parishioners.

They had a need, they had faith; they asked, and they received. What happened at Nag's Head in the twentieth century seemed no whit stranger to them than what had happened at Cana in the first century when another very real need arose at a wedding feast.

14
THE PHANTOM SCHOONER

The night of February 1, 1921, was a relatively quiet one at Cape Hatteras. The sky was overcast, but there was only a moderate onshore wind, and the keeper and crewmen of the Hatteras Coast Guard Station expected a routine watch. No lights of passing ships were visible to the lookout, and no signals of distress were observed. In the quiet hours before dawn there was not the slightest hint that the next few hours were to bring events that would be talked about to this day and would throw the Department of the Navy, the Department of Commerce, and the Justice Department of the United States into extended investigations lasting many months but leading exactly nowhere.

As the hours of that night wore away toward dawn and the eastern sky began to show the first faint shade of lighter darkness, the lookout on duty scanned once again the full one-hundred-and-eighty-degree arc from north to south where he knew the horizon to be. Seeing no sign of any vessel, he turned to the ever-ready pot for a bracing cup of hot, black coffee.

Upon turning back to the brightening sea, he started

violently, looked away, blinked his eyes, and then stared again in disbelief at the sight before him.

There, on the surface of the relatively calm sea and stuck fast on the sand shoal known as the Outer Diamond, was one of the biggest and most beautiful schooners he had ever seen. A five-masted queen of the seas she was, with every canvas—up to the topsail and out to the farthermost jib—set and drawing beautifully as though she were sailing before the lightest of breezes. By telescope the lookout could see the large ship being driven harder and harder aground by every wave running shoreward before the freshening wind. He could see no one on her deck.

He gave the alarm, and the Coastguardsmen tumbled out of their bunks and dashed outside, dressing as they ran. Daylight had increased now, and the ship was plainly visible from the porches of the station. The incredulous surfmen, with expressions of wonder, prepared their motor surfboat and launched it through the small breakers to go to the aid of the grounded craft. She had given no distress signal, and she gave none now as the surfboat came nearer.

The shoaly, turbulent water of the Outer Diamond made trying to board her inadvisable unless absolutely necessary, and, besides, no invitation had been received to come aboard. Under the laws of the sea, you just don't go barging onto the ship of another man unless he specifically invites you or unless he is obviously in danger and needs your assistance. If a man's house is his castle, then a captain's ship is his kingdom, and no one may cross its borders without his express consent or invitation. This, mind you, applies to the smallest charter boat as strongly as to the largest ocean liner.

Keeping a respectful distance, the Coast Guard boat proceeded to circle this strange visitor and to hail her loudly. No reply came from the nearly motionless vessel, and no life stirred on her deck. Except for the gentle action of the waves, she might well have been "a painted ship upon a painted ocean." As they passed around her stern, they could see her name painted in large letters upon her transom: *Carroll M. Deering*. She was obviously almost brand-new, and there was not a tear nor even a patch on any of her sails.

High out of the water but in nearly level trim she sat, in deathly, eerie silence and without any sign of life. Even the hardy Coastguardsmen, used as they were to the mysteries of the sea, could feel cold chills run up and down their spines as they lay off in deeper water and stared at this ghostly ship.

Since apparently the ship was in no immediate danger, the Coastguardsmen returned to shore and reported to the station keeper, who tried to determine from the naval register whose ship she was and whence she came. It was quickly discovered that she was, indeed, a new ship, only recently launched in the State of Maine. The listed owners were immediately notified by telegraph, and, before breakfast was over, a request came back from the owners that a boarding party be sent to the *Deering* to try to determine what was wrong.

Returning through the now-increasing surf—this time steering directly for the strange ship—the motor launch lay close alongside and under power in the choppy sea while, one by one, the crew scrambled aboard the *Deering*, leaving only the helmsman and one apprentice surfman on the launch to fend off and stand by. Since the day was unseasonably warm, the entire crew were barefoot, and most of them were hatless.

As they mounted the ship's wooden ladder and eased themselves over her portside rail, the Coastguardsmen proceeded to gather in a group, not afraid but apprehensive, every sense alert and taut in anticipation.

There was a silence on that deck and a sense of foreboding that made men look quickly behind them from time to time as though to catch anybody or anything that might be slipping up on them, but nothing was forthcoming. After a while, the men began to grin a little sheepishly at one another and to relax just a bit. They broke into groups of twos and threes and began a fine-toothed examination of the ship.

They went down into the crew's quarters and found everything neatly stowed away. The captain's cabin and the mate's lodgings were as neat and clean as though they had been prepared for an inspection. Even the spirits locker in the captain's cabin was untouched, although it was unlocked, which was thought to be unusual. They found inside it an ample supply of whisky and other spirits normally carried for medicinal purposes upon such ships. Search as they might, however, the boarding party could discover no sextant, no quadrant, and no telescope. Both the mate's and the captain's quarters were devoid of any navigational instruments whatsoever, and all the charts for the Middle Atlantic coast were missing. These apparently had not been torn out or snatched from among the other charts; they were just absent. There was no trace of the ship's logbook.

It was about this time that the searchers below decks began to be conscious of a rhythmic motion of the ship's hull, a muffled banging at the ship's stern, and the sound of freshening wind in the rigging topside. They knew instantly that the weather was beginning to "breeze up" and that they must finish their examination promptly.

In the ship's dining saloon the mystery deepened. There on the dinner table was a complete meal set out to be eaten. Each of the plates had been served, and there was food also in the serving dishes in the middle of the table. From all appearances not one mouthful had been consumed from the plates, but there was no disarray, nothing spilled. In the galley there was more food in the cooking utensils on the stove. The pots were cold, and the galley fire had gone out, but there the food was, ready to be served.

It was here that the searchers found the only living thing on board. From behind the galley stove, almost startling the men out of their wits, came a large, gray cat, in obvious good health and seemingly very glad to have human company once again.

Meanwhile, on deck, the wind was continuing to freshen. It was only as the Coastguardsmen prepared to leave that they noticed that all the ship's lifeboats were missing. Also missing were the large anchors which should have hung at her bow. The muffled banging at the stern was now identified as that of the ship's rudder slapping back and forth in the increasing waves—but the steering wheel hung motionless before the binnacle. This phenomenon was quickly explained, however, when it was found that the heavy rope cables that had connected the wheel with the rudder had been severed by what must have been a single, powerful blow from a heavy, sharp instrument, such as an axe. This left the wheel unresponsive to the flapping of the rudder.

One other sign of force or violence was found. On the broad, portside rail, just where the ship's wooden ladder had been placed overside, there was a very deep cut, apparently made by the same instrument that had severed the ship's steering cables.

The *Carroll M. Deering* was a ghost ship, a vessel without anchors, without a means of steering, without navigational aids, and without lifeboats. She was inching harder and harder aground on the treacherous shoal with every wave that struck her stern, and the wind and waves were increasing by the minute. It was time to go. Taking along the cat (which was promptly named Carroll), they hurried overside and into the waiting motor launch. They circled the *Deering* once more and then headed back inshore to their station.

Word was flashed immediately not only to the *Carroll Deering*'s owners but also to the other Coast Guard stations up and down the beach regarding this most mysterious happening. By order of the Commandant in Norfolk, an intensive search was begun by all stations located on that part of the Atlantic shore line. On foot and on horseback, land-based patrols made a thorough examination all along the edges of the various sounds as well as that of the ocean. Other men in patrol boats carefully covered the shore lines. For miles both to the north and to the south of Hatteras—all the way from Caffey's Inlet in the north to Beaufort Inlet in the south—every cove, every bay, every inlet, every foot of shore line was searched for survivors or for even some piece of wreckage of the lifeboats of the *Deering*.

The search went on for days but turned up nothing. No bodies, no piece of seagoing gear that could possibly have come from the lifeboats, no evidence that the boats had been burned on or near the beaches was ever found. It seemed as though the captain, mate, and crew of the ghost ship had arisen from a hearty meal without tasting the food, had launched the lifeboats, and had sailed away into eternity with no further sign or trace. No member of that crew ever turned up at home, and not one was ever heard from again, so far as is known.

The luckless ship was too hard aground to be salvaged, and no effort was made to free her. The owners gave instructions that she be stripped of her canvas, rigging, supplies, and anything else of value that could be removed. She was then to be abandoned, right where she was, to break up under the gales and storms that often sweep this shoaly graveyard of so many splendid craft. All this was done, and the hulk was duly listed on all charts as a possible menace to navigation. Her exact position was noted, and it was hoped that she would serve as a sort of super spar buoy to warn passing vessels of the deadly shoal of the Outer Diamond.

Abandoned she was, but the *Carroll Deering* was far from forgotten. Ashore, the story of the phantom ship and the missing crew had set tongues to wagging all up and down the seaboard. Piracy was strongly suspected. The inevitable cry was raised, "Why doesn't the government do something?" So insistent became this demand for official action that many high officials in various branches of the federal government took an intense interest. Separate investigations were launched by the Justice Department, the Commerce Department, and the Department of the Navy. After all, who would want to go to sea when such a thing as this could happen and yet remain unexplained right on our own doorstep? The mystery certainly needed solving from many standpoints, and determined efforts to unravel it were begun.

The vanished captain had had an excellent reputation as an honest and thoroughly capable master, and it was thought highly unlikely that the mishap, if mishap there had been, was caused by his negligence. His daughter moved down from Massachusetts and besieged the Justice Department to find her father or, at least, to solve the mystery of his disappearance. She was convinced that piracy was the explanation.

As if to pile mystery upon mystery, a short time after she had made her representations to the Justice Department, a bottle was washed ashore on Cape Hatteras. Inside the bottle was a message that told of a swift pirate attack and of survivors set adrift in open lifeboats with no oars or other means of locomotion. Although the note was unsigned and although the *Carroll Deering* was not named, the captain's daughter was sure she recognized the handwriting as being that of a crewman whom she knew. By permission of the finders, the bottle and the message were turned over to the Justice Department.

A very thorough backtracking was begun on the *Carroll M. Deering*, and several very interesting facts were brought to light. One of her crew, it was discovered, had been a Finn. Now that was enough, right there, in the minds of some to explain the eerie happenings. Old tales were revived of the ancient superstitions about Finnish sailors and their ability to whistle up a wind and do divers other weird and occult things aboard ship. Some of the more ancient shore-bound mariners told blood-chilling stories of other phantom ships they had heard of. There were tales of the souls of luckless sailors doomed to serve forever under the command of a phantom Finn, sailing on a voyage that could never end but must last through all eternity, with never another glimpse of home or loved ones. Their fate: only the endless, rolling, monotonous, cruel sea forever—and forever—and forever.

As the multiple official investigations got under way, it was learned that the original captain of the *Deering* had been taken violently ill just after the ship had left Newport News on her way to Rio de Janeiro with a cargo of coal. The sick man had been removed to a hospital, and a new captain put aboard to continue the journey. This, too, had seemed a bad omen, but the schooner had made the trip to South America without undue incident. The cargo of coal was unloaded in Rio, and, after the usual shore leave, the crew under the capable command of the new master sailed the ship smartly back to the British island of Barbados in the West Indies. Here the captain was to pick up orders and, possibly, a new cargo.

Port was made in Bridgetown on Barbados, and it was here that the mystery really began to evolve. Granted liberty ashore, the crew became involved in several waterfront brawls, and, for some reason, there was dark talk of "doing in" the new captain. These threats were discovered later by at least two of the investigating departments, although it must be admitted that the informants questioned were not all of the highest moral character and that most were regular habitués of the waterfront saloons of that colorful town. It should be noted, too, that Barbados rum has for generations been famous for its property of generating wild talk and vague threats against all authority. At any rate, no new cargo was picked up at Bridgetown, and orders were received for the *Deering* to return, empty, to Newport News.

The official investigations disclosed that the schooner left Bridgetown with the flood tide on January 9, 1921. At that time, although she rode rather high in the water because of her empty holds, she appeared to be in good shape. She left with a fair wind and under full sail with clear skies. No one had jumped ship, in spite of the ominous talk, and, as the vessel headed out from the harbor entrance for the open sea, she had her normal complement of eight able-bodied seamen, plus her captain and mate. It was remembered that she was handled well as she left the island. Her sails were well trimmed and drawing, and the helmsman brought her along nicely. The *Carroll M. Deering* was a beautiful sight, they say, with her brand-new, snow-white sails reaching skyward and the blue homeward-bound pennant waving at the very top of her mizzenmast. She soon acquired a "bone in her teeth" of white foam around her forefoot as she gathered speed for her homing.

On January 23, the *Deering* hailed the Cape Fear lightship just off the port of Wilmington, North Carolina. The officer of the watch reported that all was well and requested that word of her progress be sent by the lightship to Newport News. The lightship logged her as sailing smartly and appearing in excellent condition.

Then, for six full days and nights, nothing was heard of the *Deering*. It was January 29 before she was sighted by Cape Lookout lightship, only some seventy miles northwardly of the Cape Fear lightship. She should have been making much better speed than that.

As the *Deering* passed Cape Lookout lightship, generally referred to as the "Southern Gateway to the Graveyard of the Atlantic," the duty officer of the lightship observed that most of the schooner's crew appeared to be lolling about her deck in idleness. The man standing at her wheel hailed the lightship and reported that the *Deering* had lost both her anchors in a storm. He asked that other ships be requested to give her a wide berth for that reason. Even at the time, this seemed strange because there had been no storm reported anywhere along the coast and the mystery ship was under full sail and moving swiftly along to the northward.

After the Cape Lookout sighting, nothing was heard from her again until she was discovered aground on the Outer Diamond. From Lookout onward all the investigations ran into a void, as empty as the surface of the sea itself. So far as the Navy, the Coast Guard, and the Justice and Commerce Departments are concerned, that was the last time the crew of the phantom ship was seen alive.

The stripped and stranded schooner broke in two during the next full gale that swept the coast. The stern half of the ship came ashore almost intact and within

a few days was taken over by great flocks of sea gulls, fish hawks, and other noisy and quarrelsome sea birds. So thickly did these birds populate the wreck and so constant was their quarreling, crying, and wailing that the residents of the area petitioned the government to do something to destroy or abate the nuisance.

Even the nights were made hideous by the constant crying of the birds. The insane merriment of a score of laughing gulls at midnight can prove nerve-wracking to the hardiest of Bankers. They wanted an end put to this distracting situation as soon as possible. In their dilemma they turned to the Coast Guard for assistance.

The pleas of these beleagured people were heard, and two Coast Guard cutters were ordered to Norfolk. There they were loaded with explosives to be carried to Hatteras. It was calculated that two boatloads of explosives should be enough to destroy the noisy stern section of the troublesome schooner.

Before the cutters could load and leave the dock, however, one of those sudden northeast storms for which Hatteras is famous sprang up and saved them the trouble. The tremendous surf literally beat the wreck to pieces, scattering planks and lumber for miles along the coast, to the enrichment of many an honest beachcomber who was in need of just such a plank or post for use in or around his house. Many of these planks remain to this day as portions of those houses and are considered by many to insure the best possible luck.

Thus did the *Carroll M. Deering* come to her end, but there are those who say that the breaking up of the wreck and the scattering of the laughing gulls did nothing to remedy the really frightening noises along that stretch of beach. Particularly in time of storm—and especially during a February storm—some insist that you need only listen to hear shrieks and moans of human voices carried on the wind; that the only distinguishable words sound like some desperate soul crying over and over again through the storm and the wind, "Find us—— Fiiiind us——Ohhhhhhhhhhhhhh find us!"

15
THE BOOZHYOT

South of Portsmouth Island on the Outer Banks lies the elongated strip of sand known as Core Banks. This barrier of low-lying beach runs in a southwesterly direction and terminates in a thumb-shaped peninsula known as Point or Cape Lookout. From the base of this thumb the Outer Banks then run almost northwest and are known as Shackleford Banks. Between Cape Lookout and Shackleford Banks is Barden's Inlet, a thoroughfare for many of the fishing boats of the area on their way from Sound-based berths to the open sea. On Cape Lookout stands one of the most familiar lighthouses of the Atlantic coast. Painted white with black diamonds, Cape Lookout Light warns northbound ships that they are approaching the deadly Diamond Shoals, Graveyard of the Atlantic.

The people of Portsmouth Island, Core Banks, and Shackleford Banks share close blood ties and a common philosophical outlook with the other Outer Bankers. The families have intermarried, and there are many bonds of friendship, as well as kinship, which unite these people into one ethnic whole. They are all, in the very finest sense of the word, Outer Bankers.

The exact locale of this story is Cape Lookout, but not all of the participants were Lookouters—which is as far as any of them shall be identified for reasons that will presently appear. You may be quite sure that any name used in this story is not the name of a person who has ever lived, so far as the writer knows. If there is such a person with such a name, it is purely coincidence and nothing more.

It was the winter of 1930, and the country lay stunned in the nearly full paralysis of the Great Depression. Bread lines grew longer in the cities, and as the winter deepened, privations became ever more acute. There was suffering in many places, and some families actually went hungry at times. These were the days of the Al Capones, the Legs Diamonds, and the Dutch Schultzes. These were also the days of vicious gang wars and of big-time rumrunners.

The Great Depression had come to the coastland of North Carolina, too. Along the Outer Banks the always uncertain chances of fishing were made even more tenuous by the low prices paid for the fish. True, some wealthy sportsmen still came down for the duck and goose hunting, but they were far fewer than before. Some of the Bankers even took to yaupon harvesting in an effort to ease the bitter pinch. The spirit of the people never broke, though; and the wry jokes, the broad humor, and the indomitable courage of these thorough-bred coastal inhabitants stood them in good stead. They survived.

One February night in the dark of the moon, when the sky was so black that the stars looked for all the world like diamonds spilled on black velvet, an event happened which was to burn itself into the folklore and the very vocabulary of the region. The sea was quiet that night—as quiet as a sleeping woman—with only the slow, regular breath-like sigh of gentle wavelets spending themselves on the coarse shell gravel. No sea bird broke the stillness, and no trace of wind disturbed the graceful sea oats that crowned the small dunes and filled the shoreward hollows.

It must have been just about dead low tide when Clemmie Liverman from Harker's Island was putting out through Barden's Inlet to make his way to the fishing grounds at sea. One of the Liverman boys had only the day before finished work on a powerful searchlight and installed it on the Liverman fishing boat. Clemmie himself did not think much of the light, but the boy had worked long and hard at putting it together and installing it. Maybe it would be of some use in spotting buoys after dark or in assisting other fishing boats that might be in trouble. At any rate, there it was, bolted securely to the pilothouse and out of the way of the nets and their running gear.

At the same time, running southward along the eastern shore of Cape Lookout and approaching the point of that Cape was a low, sleek craft, a rumrunner or smuggler from the fleet owned and operated by one of the biggest and most ruthless of the top gangsters. Low in the water she rode as though heavily laden, her powerful twin motors muffled to a steady throb, her running lights extinguished. At her wheel a harried-looking man in a skipper's cap peered through the darkness, looking for the lights of Morehead City and anxious at all events to avoid an inquisitive Coast Guard or Revenue cutter. He was not bound for Morehead City. He was headed south and wanted only to get by the Carolina coast unobserved. Already Lookout lighthouse was just abaft his starboard beam.

It was at this moment that Clemmie Liverman turned the point of Lookout. No sooner had he cleared it than he made out in the darkness the unmistakable bow-wave of another boat headed directly for him on a collision course and, more than that, without running lights. Shouting a hoarse warning, Clemmie put his helm hard over and jammed his throttle wide open to accelerate his boat out of harm's way. For once, the old engine responded with a surge of power that Clemmie had not suspected was in her. With a roar that would have done credit to an airplane engine, the old fishing boat literally surged ahead. Simultaneously, Clemmie bethought him of the searchlight. With one twist of the handle and one flick of the switch, he threw all the electrical power being generated by that wildly racing motor into a splendid beam of light that caught and held the rum-running yacht in a brilliant spot of illumination. Every detail of her stood out as plainly as though it were mid-day.

Aboard the gangster's yacht immediate and total consternation ensued. One voice, louder than the rest of the shouting, seemed to come from someone in command. "Jesu," it shouted, "the——federals!" Then, with a note of panic, "Get rid of it! Get rid of it! Lighten ship, damn your eyes. Lighten ship, and let's get out of here. You want to *die*?" There came the powerful roar of twin motors, suddenly strained to the maximum of their capacity. There was even the harsh, staccato sound of machinegun fire, the red streaks of tracer bullets which sprayed toward the searchlight, and, immediately, the sound of splashing alongside the swiftly turning yacht. With a crash of broken glass, the searchlight on the Liverman boat went suddenly dark. The machinegun had found its target. Luckily, Clemmie Liverman was not even scratched, but, scared out of his wits, he put his helm even farther over, made a complete circle, and ran for the cover of Barden's Inlet. He made it, too, and got back to Harker's Island, but it was more than a week before he was up to going out again in his trusty boat. The rumrunning yacht, meanwhile, had turned back north and, heedless of the threatening shoals, had fled at breakneck speed into the darkness.

The Bankers, startled out of a deep sleep by the sudden bedlam, had not been hasty about showing a light or venturing out on the beach. Some of them remembered all too well the deadly sound of a machinegun. Many of them had heard that sound from the trenches in Belgium and from the decks of Naval vessels in the first World War.

However, when the roar of motors had died away to the north, the machinegun fire had stopped, and the beach was quiet again under the wink–wink–wink of Lookout light flashing as regularly as ever, some of the bolder of the Bankers ventured out with lanterns and flashlights. After all, someone might be in need of help. They searched the beach, but the night now seemed as calm and peaceful as before. Over in the Sound someone was punishing a fishing-boat motor, but even that was fading into the distance. The beach itself was as flat and clean as a recent storm tide had washed it. After a brief survey of the shore line and a long look and listen seaward, the hastily clad Bankers began to be aware of the cold, and, one by one, they made their ways back to the warm comfort of their respective beds. So far as they could determine, nothing of an unusual nature was to be found on the beach, and whoever had made all the ruckus had departed into the night.

There are always a number of people awake and about at daybreak on the Outer Banks, whatever the season and whatever the weather. Many of these early birds are youngsters. Like youngsters everywhere, these Outer Banks kids are among the world's best watchers and finders. Like their inland counterparts, they are the ones who invariably know what is going on, where, and why. It was not unusual, therefore, that, at daybreak after the noisy night before, a youth of about twelve years (whose name certainly was not Horatio Gillikin, but whom we shall call by that name because we like the ring of it) was already roused, dressed, combed, fed, and turned out of the house to meander along the strand.

As he engaged in that priceless heritage and prerogative of youth to dawdle, loiter, fool, and mess around with nowhere in particular to go and all day long to get there, his attention was suddenly arrested by an unusual lump or bulge on the beach which had certainly not been there the afternoon before. Used as he was to all sorts of strange things washing up from the sea, Horatio approached the strange object cautiously and with every sense alert, until he perceived in the growing light of sunrise that it was inanimate and was one of several score such objects scattered along the beach.

On closer examination this newly arrived phenomenon turned out to be a burlap bag, better known in the

area as a croaker-sack, of roughly the size that super-
markets use to hold large grocery orders. Protruding
from the partially-open neck of this bag were several
sizable bunches of straw. Nestled in the bag, but kept
from contact with each other by the straw packing,
were four rather large bottles. It took but an instant
to cut the string that loosely secured the top of the bag
and to withdraw therefrom one of the bottles, which
was wrapped in some sort of tissue paper. After remov-
ing the wrapper, the young lad—who was not named
Horatio Gillikin—squinted earnestly in the still inade-
quate dawn light to read the label on the bottle. There
was a picture on the label of a large and splendid white
horse which stood out quite clearly, and underneath
the picture were printed some words and figures:

"Estab. 1742." Above the horse were other words that had become quite obliterated by sea water, and, finally, down and to the right, an inscription: "86.8 Proof."

Mystified by the cryptic words and picture and yet almost consumed with curiosity about what treasure he had found, our young non-Horatio managed to pry off the foil and open the bottle, only to find that the smell emanating from it was as mysterious as its label. Then, with the same courage that drove Columbus ever westward and John Glenn ever skyward and with the same self-sacrificing spirit of curiosity that prompted Pasteur to expose himself to rabies and that ancient unknown hero to swallow the first oyster, our lad put the strange bottle to his lips, tilted back his head, and took a giant swallow.

Some five minutes later, when he had stopped coughing, retching, and sneezing; when he had put out most of the fire in his mouth and throat with cool sea water and had, to some degree, regained his equilibrium and composure, our experimenter took drastic revenge. Once again he picked up the treacherous bottle and proceeded to fling it just as far toward the ocean as his strength would permit. The bottle turned over and over, spilling liquid as it flew, and finally descended with a satisfying plunk into the deep water just beyond the first sand bar. Horatio had just turned around to start back home when he bethought himself of the possibility that perhaps, after all, he had found something that might be of value. Surely some adult would know for what use it was intended. Never once did it cross his mind that the stuff in these bottles might be whisky. He had seen and smelled the "white lightning" or bootleg whisky that some of the older men had in small quantities from time to time, but this stuff in the horse bottle was entirely different, in his opinion. Returning to the beach, he picked up the bag with the remaining three bottles inside and, slinging it over his shoulder, started for home.

There has always been, and there remains to this day, among the people of the Outer Banks one of the swiftest and most dependable systems of communication the world has ever seen. Although these Islanders were to some degree remote from the rest of the world, there was, and still is, a closeness among them, a mutuality of interest that makes them almost clairvoyant in the exchange of information. As a "grapevine," it has no equal. Thus, it was only a very short period of time after Horatio's find had been identified as bottled-in-bond Scotch whisky before practically all of the Islanders had the news.

With this key piece of the puzzle in hand, it was easy for the Islanders to see what had happened. A big-time rumrunner, as he was called in those days, had for some reason been "spooked" or mistakenly led to believe that he had been intercepted by one of the fast submarine chasers the federal government had converted into Revenue cutters for the express purpose of running down smugglers. It had been the sound of this rumrunner's flight that had disturbed the Islanders' rest the night before. Since it was common knowledge on the Island that the government cutter, normally based at Beaufort, had gone to Charleston for repairs, there was no apparent reason for the headlong flight of the rumrunner, unless perhaps highjackers had ambushed him.

Whatever the reason, it was obvious to the Bankers that the rumrunner had had to jettison a large portion of his cargo in order to effect a rapid escape up the shallow slough that ran northward along the beach. Most of the luxury boats engaged in smuggling whisky into the country in those days were deserving of the appellation "yacht." Sleek, fast, and beautiful, they were provided with large holds for the storage of contraband— the kind of dream boat the average fisherman hears about but sees only rarely. Capacious as they were, however, when loaded they drew too much water to cross the outer sand bar, which is always present just offshore in that region.

Well, when thieves fall out, honest men prosper. The Bankers converged on that portion of the beach where the bottled-in-bond Scotch had come ashore and helped themselves. There were more than enough bottles to go around, and soon everybody who had the notion also had the wherewithal. No one took more than his fair share. Characteristically, they shared with each other. Of course, since some of them didn't drink, there was no point in their taking any. Since others did not want their wives to know they were interested, a number of quick deals were made, whereby one would take custody of another's share—but that fooled nobody. Everybody knew exactly what was going on and what was going to happen. They watched it develop with the same apprehensive but fatalistic fascination with which they would have watched the approach of a tidal wave.

What did happen was one of the biggest, wildest wing-dings ever seen in that section. Those who did not partake tried their best to go about their business as usual. Those who did partake, partook with a vengeance. Groups of revelers strode about in happy abandon, hailing one another and whooping it up in general.

As the day flowed on, a sort of password or countersign sprang up. As one group would approach another, someone would shout, "Hey, mate, where'd you get your liquor?" The reply, usually shouted in unison by the other group, was "From the booze-yacht, mate. From the booze-yacht." Of course, in good time the words became more and more slurred. By midafternoon the commonly accepted pronunciation was "Boozhyot," or in some cases "Boozy-Yot." The one word sufficed for both greeting and response. Remarkably, the word became funnier and funnier the more it was used and the more the mercifully soft sand pitched and weaved in apparently perfect phasing with the rolling of the sea. Oh, I tell you, mate, a good pair of sea legs stood a man in good stead that memorable afternoon.

Thus was a new two-syllable word added to the vocabulary of the Outer Banks. To this day, if a Banker tells you that he has been to a Boozhyot, he means that he has survived a party or get-together at which practically the whole group has become outrageously intoxicated, stoned, crocked, not only from the potables at hand but also from the wild spirit of abandon that characterizes a genuine Boozhyot. It is a wild thing, an uninhibited, ostentatious, orgic, Bacchanalian splurge. Thank goodness it is a rare thing. But, right or wrong, rare or frequent, Boozhyot is a part of the history of the Outer Banks.

So, if anybody ever invites you to a Boozhyot, take care, brother! You know now what you face.

16
THE BOOZHYOT APOCRYPHA

Many stories are told along the Outer Banks that are claimed to be true continuations or postscripts to the Boozhyot story. I, for one, do not believe them. They make entertaining yarns, but their spirit is foreign to the nature of the Outer Bankers. Whereas the Boozhyot story (which is related by many honorable men as a true story) reveals a sort of inherent wildness and a willingness to whoop it up as part of the character of these sturdy children of the sea, the sequels tend to intrude an element of chicanery or sneakiness, which I have never found in the character or make-up of the Outer Bankers.

Some storytellers say that the day after the original Boozhyot, when the last reveler had slept off the anesthetic portion of his indiscretion and begun to feel the inevitable hangover, a great many bottles of Scotch remained intact in the burlap bags. There had just been more liquor than there were imbibers. One Boozhyot had apparently been enough to last the participants for several years, because few, if any, of the celebrants evinced any interest in the bottles that remained. Aching heads, cottony mouths, and hands that trembled so much that mending a net was out of the question were among the sobriety-inducing elements that caused the Bankers to lose interest in the remaining supply of whisky. Only the soft sand, on which most of the revelers had finally come to rest, had prevented worse injury. Only the relative balminess of the February night had averted the illnesses that might have been expected from a night under the stars.

If the repentant Bankers had lost interest, however, there were those who did find the presence of such a windfall of bottled-in-bond liquor fascinating. The cache of whisky, already ashore in the United States and unknown to the Coast Guard and to the Treasury Agents, was literally worth its weight in gold. The jeering laughter of the underworld over the unnecessary loss of such a valuable cargo had indeed been wormwood to the smugglers, and, learning of the absence of the Revenue cutter, they determined to see if there was some way to recoup.

All prospect of profit had appeared lost when the liquor-laden bags had vanished over the side of the rum-running yacht. Some of the more experienced seamen on the yacht, however, had advanced the hope that some of the cargo might have washed ashore. After all, the yacht had been very close in when it was pinpointed by that beam of light. If the cargo had survived, here was the opportunity of a lifetime to seize upon it before any rival gangs got the same idea and tried to move in. Here, in this remote location, with Prohibition the law of the land and with unslaked thirsts in Miami clamoring for the merchandise of the smugglers and willing to pay big prices—here was the chance to "get well." It was too good to pass up, and it certainly seemed worth a trip.

Three of the smugglers chartered a boat from the mainland. When they came ashore, the big one—the one with the scar running from the corner of his mouth almost to his cheek bone—spoke with a heavy Italian accent. He seemed to be the leader. The other two had little to say and stuck close to their big companion. The alert eyes of the Islanders did not miss the small bulges on the hips and under the armpits of the two silent ones. These men were obviously not fishermen—not sportsmen of any kind. The Bankers knew right away what they were. They were searchers, and their eyes were cold and hard.

Now, the true Banker does not scare easily. He has looked death in the eye many times, and mortal danger is part and parcel of his life. Usually he fears no man, but he is no fool. Naturally cautious, he will avoid danger if he can, but once he is committed, you will not find a cooler or calmer individual. When the gangsters first arrived, the Bankers did not like them, but they were not going to run from them nor lie to them, for the sooner these searchers were off the Island, the better.

Three Bankers were appointed to represent the holders of the prize. The visitors soon began negotiations for the return of the whisky to its former (if not rightful) owners. All hands freely admitted that, according to law, abandoned cargo was the rightful property of the finder but that a repurchase by the loser might be effected. Samples of unopened bottles were forthcoming to establish that the contents had not been harmed by sea water, and a price per burlap bag was finally agreed upon. Here, the rumrunners took advantage of the Bankers by setting the price far below that of the market, but the Islanders knew little of such things and went along with a price of $10.00 per parcel.

Several details of the bargain were dictated by the Bankers, however. At their insistence, the contraband was to be delivered after midnight in the dark of the moon and by small boat through the surf to the yacht, which would be lying just offshore. Further, the Islanders insisted that each bag should be passed up by one of their number to the deck of the yacht, where it would be received by another of their crew and passed down into the hold of the yacht, where yet a third Islander would stow it. The bootleggers were to have two men at the rail—one to count the bags as they came aboard, and the other to pay for them. "We might be interrupted by the Coast Guard," explained the Bankers, "and have to make a run for it in our small boat to get back to shore." All this was agreed to, and it was further stipulated that only the liquor on hand was to be expected. "After all, gentlemen, some of your liquor must still be in Davy Jones's locker. All we can let you have is what we've got."

Fortunately the night chosen for the loading of the liquor was calm as well as dark. The swift, contraband-running yacht hove to just outside the bar and waited. Promptly at midnight, the small boat of the Bankers, loaded with burlap bags, was seen putting out through what little surf there was. Rendezvous was made right on schedule, and the bootleggers extended helping hands to assist the part-time stevedores aboard. What the yacht crew did not see, however, was the two additional Islanders with soot-blackened faces who slipped quietly into the water and swam silently around to the other side of the yacht—the seaward side.

Thus the loading began. Bag by bag the liquor was passed up to the deck and then down into the hold. In the darkness of that hold, the Banker assigned to stow the cargo was being meticulously careful to stow one bag on the floor and to pass the next out the porthole, which he had opened, to his companion in the water. This worthy would take the bag, swim around the bow of the yacht, and return it to the surfboat. As he swam back toward the porthole, he would pass in the darkness his companion swimming with another bag. Once the bags were back in the surfboat, they were passed again up to the deck, counted again, paid for again, and dropped again into the hold, where one would be stowed and the next passed out the porthole again for another circuit. It was later estimated that some of those bags made as many as ten round trips before coming to a final rest in the hold of the booze yacht.

Who "caught it" for the short count when the yacht finally made port was never known. The cash received from the bamboozled counter at the rail served all through that winter to keep many a worthy Banker family in coffee and sugar. In the minds of some, this fully exemplified their ancient belief that there is some good to be realized out of almost anything.

17
"I SHALL BUT LOVE THEE BETTER AFTER DEATH"

It was September, 1933, and Amy Harris lay dying. She had lived a good life and a long one. Although her marriage had not been blessed with children, it had been one of the most successful on the entire Outer Banks. She and John had been childhood sweethearts, and their puppy love had ripened into a deep and satisfying relationship of mutual trust and love and understanding.

One summer day when they were still courting, John Harris had saved her life. Their fishing boat had sprung a sudden leak and had sunk beneath them. Swimming his ponderous but powerful breast stroke, John had plowed his way to shore and safety with Amy clinging to the back of his shoulders.

This had developed into a sort of a family tradition or joke after their marriage. Amy never learned to swim, but she often promised her husband that, given the opportunity, she would repay his heroism in kind. On these occasions he would look down into her piquantly serious little face, smile indulgently, and ask her how in the world she intended to do such a thing when she could not even swim enough to help herself. Then they would both laugh and exchange an affectionate hug or squeeze of the hand.

Most of their life had enhanced this affection. The very absence of children in their home seemed to bring them closer together, making each more considerate of the other's little whims and more devotedly aware of the other's needs and wishes. They had settled down and had bought their own little place near the village of Duck, which is quite near Caffey's Inlet on the northern reaches of North Carolina's outer strand. The fishing was good there, and just a little more than five miles of Sound separated them from the mainland of Currituck County. One could conveniently cross the Sound bridge, one of the modern improvements, to Point Harbor and then go on up to Norfolk or Elizabeth City.

In spite of all that medical science could do for her, Amy Harris died that September of 1933, slipping away peacefully while she slept. Even in the midst of his grief, John took some solace from the fact that he had been spared to look after her to the very end—"in sickness and in health till death do us part."

One of Amy's fondest wishes had been that she be "laid out" by a real undertaker when her time came and that she be buried in a concrete and steel burial vault in the little cemetery in the yaupon grove near their home. The bereaved husband, fulfilling her wish, employed the best mortician he could find in Norfolk, bought a vault, and had it shipped down in time for the funeral. Everything was to be done just as his beloved had wanted it.

All the neighbors agreed that it was a beautiful funeral and that Amy had never looked prettier. If they could have found a fault, it was that Amy looked so serious! The usual happy smile was gone from her face, and a look of almost studied seriousness had replaced it. That, however, was a minor thing, and they all congratulated John on carrying out Amy's wishes so completely. The vault was sealed and buried in the sand among the graves of other Harrises and Tates and Midgetts.

The day of the funeral, the attendants were a little nervous. They had just passed through one violent hurricane the month before, and now the Coast Guard reported a storm bigger and much more destructive than its predecessor and headed directly toward them. By the day following the funeral, the watch had become a full hurricane warning, and people were beginning to leave for the mainland. All morning long they streamed across the bridge to Point Harbor and continued further inland. Meanwhile, the wind steadily increased. By nightfall it had become a full gale, and the normally quiet Sound was a mass of whitecaps. It was certain that the full force of the tropical storm would come ashore by dawn of the next day somewhere in the vicinity of Duck and Caffey's Inlet.

In vain did John Harris' neighbors plead with him to come with them to safety on the mainland. Sere grief and an aching sense of loss were still too much with him. He had not yet really given up his Amy. She was there, and he could not and would not leave her. So great was the danger that his friends even considered taking him by force. When this also failed, they left him with his grief, notifying the Coast Guard of his lonely presence in that threatened spot. The Coast Guard immediately dispatched a beach cart to take John to safety, and the

Coastguardsmen, too, urged him to seek higher ground or to come to the station with them. To all entreaties, however, John gave the same answer. His Amy was there, and he intended to stay with her.

When the hurricane slammed ashore, she turned out to be one of the most destructive of the century. The tides rose higher and higher, sweeping across the entire outer strand of islands all along the coast. Sea water poured into the Sound through a dozen new cuts. The entire Outer Banks appeared doomed to inundation before the wild fury of a sea gone mad. The wind, screaming and wailing, was overpowering. It seemed a malevolent personality in itself, bent on destroying anything and everything in its path.

John Harris was indoors that night when the worst of it hit. The water had risen steadily around his small house to the level of his front porch. The force of the wind outside had made breathing so difficult that John had taken what refuge he could find in his cottage. Sleep was out of the question. Since the electric power had long since gone and even to attempt to light a lamp was unthinkable, there John sat, alone and in darkness. All around the house the wind howled as though ten thousand banshees straight from hell were dancing a mad, disorganized dance of death. The little house trembled like an overtaut violin string. Waves had long since beaten off the front steps, and every recurrent ocean swell striking the house threatened to sweep it away into Currituck Sound.

It must have been around midnight when John felt something heavy and solid strike the foundations of his house. Not once, but twice—three times there came a heavy, jarring thud. Struggling to his front door and opening it to the full force of the wind, John beheld to his horror a cement and steel burial vault being driven by the force of the waves against the foundations of his already shaky house.

Just at that second there occurred one of those gales within a hurricane, a gust of wind so strong that it seemed nothing could stand in its path. The entire house collapsed behind John in a welter of foam, spray, and flying, nail-studded fragments. As the porch disappeared beneath him, John flung himself atop the vault. Grasping the raised decorations on the lid, he hung on for dear life, more animal than man now in his extremity and caught up in the primordial will to live.

A concrete and steel vault is a heavy thing. It takes several strong men to move it about. But such a vault, being sealed from without, is airtight, and, although it rests low in the water and moves sluggishly with even the most violent waves and wind, it will float. John Harris, terrified and expecting each minute to be his last, clung desperately to the vault, which was literally blown that night across the width of Currituck Sound and onto some cypress knees on the mainland shore.

Search parties found him there the next day. He was sitting in knee-deep water near the burial vault, a vacant and wild look in his eyes. Although still sane, he was suffering from shock and exposure. The hair on his head, once black as a raven's wing, had turned completely white—and white it remained for the rest of his days.

The burial vault, hoisted shortly thereafter aboard a barge, was moved from the Currituck shore across the

Sound to milepost number one on the road near the village of Duck. The authorities, however, insisted that the vault and the casket within it be opened for inspection before it could be reinterred. Several of John Harris' neighbors were asked to be on hand as witnesses.

As the little crowd of reverent but interested witnesses watched, the seal was broken on the side of the vault, the top lifted off, and the casket within opened. There, sure enough, was Amy Harris. It had been her vault that had carried John across the Sound on his incredible ride. She had made good her lifelong promise to rescue her beloved if the opportunity ever arose.

The body itself was hardly disturbed; Amy looked just as she had on the day of her funeral—the same, that is, with one striking exception.

When the veil was lifted away, Amy's face was wreathed in the sweetest, the most natural-looking smile you have ever seen.

Not many years later John Harris passed on to his reward. They buried him beside his Amy in another yaupon grove and put a single tombstone over both graves.

Although John and Amy left no descendants, they are not forgotten on the Outer Banks. To this day, when the weather begins to turn ominous and the scud begins to fly before the increasing wind, residents of Duck and Caffey's Inlet will remember and will tell once again of the time John Harris' wife came back from the grave to rescue him.

18
WORD FROM THE SEA

The village of Ocracoke on Ocracoke Island of North Carolina's Outer Banks is a healthy and picturesque place in which to be and to live. It was once the haunt of the pirate Blackbeard and later the locale of the events and heroic actions that gave rise to some of the finest traditions of the United States Coast Guard as well as of the Life Saving Service. Visitors find themselves strangely attracted and attached to Ocracoke once they have experienced its quaint and restful calm. Its native sons and daughters love it with a fierce and sincere passion. By and large, Ocracokers are a serene, courageous, and noble people, and life on their island can be a happy idyl.

Such people were Bill and Annie Gaskill, who lived in Ocracoke during the 1920's, the depression thirties, and the war-torn forties. Bill and Annie operated a modern and spotlessly clean hostelry known as the Pamlico Inn. Facing the broad and usually calm waters of Pamlico Sound some distance from Ocracoke Inlet, it was the sort of place to which people "in the know" returned year after year for long-remembered visits. Its regular patrons became almost a family in their own right. The unhurried days of island life and the peaceful, star-spangled nights wove a magic spell, and it was an insensitive person indeed who did not succumb to the enchantment.

As an adjunct to the Inn, there was, of course, a wharf or pier, which extended from the shore out into the deeper water of the Sound. To this convenience were tied all kinds of small boats. From time to time there were sailboats, motor boats, trawlers, and purse-seiners; there were crab boats, shad boats, and dories both with and without motors. All were welcome to use the Pamlico Inn wharf.

Bill and Annie Gaskill had a son whom they had named James Baum Gaskill soon after his birth in 1916. As a boy and as a young man, this son dearly loved to spend his time on and around those boats secured to the pier. Here he learned to swim, to sail, and to tell the difference between a hard-shelled crab and a "peeler" before darting his hand down into the water to pick up the crustacean. The boy displayed early an intense interest in and capacity for navigation, seamanship, and the mechanics of internal-combustion engines. He became an accomplished boatman and capable navigator at an early age.

Of a naturally sunny disposition, Jim was known and accepted by the Ocracokers as one of their very own. There was not a home on the Island where he was not welcome and where he did not feel free to show up at mealtime or party time almost as though he were blood kin to the owners. They knew him and loved him, and he knew and loved them, too. They depended on each other. People of the Island were as sure of Jim—of his courage, his honesty, and his loyalty—as they were of their own right hands. They relied upon him, and he upon them, and each justified the faith of the other. No Scottish clan was ever closer knit, no band of knights more fiercely loyal.

To Jim, the sea was a way of life. That ocean near his doorstep was always referred to as "she" or "her," never as "it" or "that." The sea was both a generous mother and a raging she-devil, depending on her mood. In her moments of sunny calm, she was life-giving, providing the very food the Islanders ate and serving as the broad highway on which they traveled to the outside world. In her moments of terrible anger, she was a cross-grained, terrible witch to be treated with respect and a healthy but cautious admiration—but never with fear. Although the Bankers may stay ashore in time of storm and gale, they show not the slightest hesitation in putting out in their small boats if such becomes necessary to the saving of human life. So strongly is this feeling ingrained in them that they see nothing remarkable about it. It is the expected thing, a sort of natural and instinctive *noblesse oblige*, and they do not feel comfortable in a boat with anyone who does not share this feeling.

One of the proudest traditions of the area is the reply that a grizzled Coast Guard captain gave to a young recruit who asked fearfully whether the boat crew could expect to return alive if they put out through the raging sea on the rescue mission to which they had been called. "Son," replied the Skipper, "there is nothing in the manual that says we have to return. It only says we have to go."

Of such a philosophy was Jim Baum Gaskill. He was one with his fellow Islanders in spirit and in outlook, and it was the most natural thing imaginable that he should turn to the sea for his living and his livelihood. He applied himself to learning all the seamanship obtainable in this place of professional mariners, and he grew steadily in stature and in understanding.

At the time of the treacherous Japanese attack on Pearl Harbor in December, 1941, Jim had already earned his master's license and was a qualified and experienced ship captain. How could he better serve his country in this hour of her need than by joining the Merchant Marine to help keep the lines of supply open? His application for service was gladly accepted by the United States War Shipping Board, and he was assigned to the vessel *Carib Sea*, one of the few freighters immediately available to carry on the dangerous wartime commerce. The *Carib Sea* was not a fighting vessel. She was slow, fat, and clumsy, but she could do the job for which she was built and could help to fill a need more urgent than most Americans knew. A machinegun on her foredeck and a hastily installed small cannon on her stern comprised her only armament and her sole protection during her assigned travels in the offshore waters of the eastern seaboard.

This, then, was the vessel on which Captain Jim Gaskill sailed in the service of his country. In early March, 1942, he directed her at her best cruising speed southwardly on the edge of the Gulf Stream and somewhere between the Point of Hatteras and the then-friendly island of Cuba.

Official weather records show that, on Ocracoke Island on March 11 of that year, a typical northeast gale began to blow. It was a storm of violent proportions and intensity but one the like of which the Islanders had seen many times before. It was a raging, howling full gale, but since the Islanders have seen many a hurricane, they do not bother too much about a full gale. When it had blown itself out, as such storms always do, there was the inevitable cleaning up to do. Bill Gaskill went out on his wharf, as was his custom after such storms, to see what, if any, damage had been done to his pier or to the boats alongside. There was the expected small damage to the minor piling of the structure, and some of the boats appeared half full of Sound water, but no real damage was apparent, and Bill started to go back toward Pamlico Inn.

As he turned, he became aware of a rather large plank which the wavelets of the incoming tide were beating against the weather-piling of his pier. It appeared to be a black board some eight or ten feet in length and possibly two feet in width. Taking a boathook from a nearby skiff, Bill placed the point of the hook against the board and pushed down to propel it out and around the end of the wharf so that it would float free with the tide. No sooner had the board cleared the reach of the boathook than the force of the waves returned it to the piling, where it began to beat once more against the slender supports. Exasperated, Bill obtained the necessary leverage on the offending board by placing the boathook underneath the edge of the floating timber and across the flooring of the pier. With an expert twist he then

flipped it out of the water and up onto the deck of his wharf.

When the water-sogged board tumbled onto the deck, the side that had been under water was turned up to the sunlight and to Bill's incredulous and horrified gaze. There, in large gilt letters on the board, were the words: *Carib Sea*. It was, indeed, the nameplate from the very ship on which his son Jim Baum Gaskill had sailed and on which—as later official information confirmed—Jim had lost his life when she was torpedoed and sunk.

Neither Bill Gaskill, nor his wife Annie, nor any other Ocracoker seemed particularly amazed that this one board should travel up the Gulf Stream in the broad Atlantic, enter Jim Baum Gaskill's home inlet, and conclude by beating against the supports of the very pier on which Jim had played as a boy. Jim Baum Gaskill had belonged to the sea, as they all did, and it was not particularly remarkable that the sea should bring news of the death of one of her own.

Later that same afternoon one of Jim's brothers happened to be walking along the ocean shore, observing bits and pieces of wreckage that were being washed up in the wake of the storm. The tears in his young eyes may have resulted from the sharp wind, or they may have been for the brother he would never see again, but they did not blind his vision against a particularly large piece of wreckage in the wash. On the beach just opposite the Pamlico Inn there had come ashore, intact, the door from the pilothouse of the *Carib Sea*. To that door were secured the licenses of several of the officers of the vessel and, among them, the master's license of Captain

James B. Gaskill. Once again Mother Sea was bringing word to her children of the passing of one of the best and brightest of her sons.

It was weeks later when the War Department sent word to Bill and Annie Gaskill of the loss of their son in the line of duty at sea. By then it was old news to Bill and Annie, as indeed it was to the other residents of Ocracoke. The sea had already brought them word. They knew they could trust the sea. So well did they trust her that they had already held a beautiful and simple memorial ceremony in honor of their departed friend, and Jim had become by then another of the glowing legends of the heroic fraternity of Outer Bankers. Already they had besought their God for a peaceful rest for their beloved Captain Jim Baum Gaskill.

To this day, in the United Methodist Church in Ocracoke Village on Ocracoke Island, Hyde County, North Carolina, there rests upon the altar a beautiful, gold-colored cross. Upon the base of the cross may be observed an inscription, which reads: IN MEMORY OF CAPT. JAMES B. GASKILL. JULY 2, 1916. MARCH 11, 1942. THIS CROSS CONSTRUCTED FROM SALVAGE OF THE SHIP UPON WHICH CAPTAIN GASKILL LOST HIS LIFE.

Thus do the Islanders of Ocracoke accept with simple trust events that might prove amazing to people of less faith. Thus do they accept with resignation and with belief in the goodness of God the stark fact that, long before the government sent official word to the Gaskills, the sea brought the news to Ocracoke that Jim Baum Gaskill had made the supreme sacrifice for his country.

It is with many an eye fixed on this memorial cross that these Islanders sometimes sing in their Sunday worship services the words of that glorious old hymn:

> For all in danger on the stormy deep,
> For all who 'neath their billows sleep,
> Great God of wave and wind and sky
> Thy boundless mercy now we seek.